WARRIOR RISING

WARRIOR RISING

THE WOMARA SERIES
BOOK TWO

J. L. NICELY

For information address JLNicely.com

For permissions address Braintree Press c/o JLNicely.com

Published September 2019

Published in the United States of America

ISBN: 978-1-7321010-2-9 pbk

ISBN: 978-1-7321010-3-6 ebk

Library of Congress Control Number: 9781732101029

Cover Art by Godfrey Escota

There is cry upon the wind to all women, that makes the warrior within us shout out, that we will never go back. These are those times...

Also by J.L. Nicely

The Womara Series
Book One: Unconquered Warrior

CONTENTS

1

HOMEWARD BOUND

Storm clouds gathered quickly and the sea churned an inky black as Seanna clung to the rail, steadying herself against the lurching boat while another wave crashed over the deck. The swell of the water lifted the bow, then dropped the boat from the top of the crest. She gripped the rail more tightly and braced herself for another impact as she watched the rolling waves, which only the day before had been smooth as glass.

The center sails flapped furiously, loosened by the gusts that drove the ship down the coastline toward the port of Lord Edmond, at the southern tip of her homeland. The boat's crew moved quickly along the deck, securing sails and cargo. Seanna caught the men's sideways glances and quick smirks to one another as she speculated that they were enjoying her discomfort, but she ignored them as she widened her stance and kept herself steady against the bow.

I refuse to give anyone the satisfaction of watching me retch

*over the side. No storm or the prospect of seasickness can dampen
my excitement. I am heading home!*

Seanna closed her eyes against the stinging rain that began to
fall as she invoked an image of her deep, quiet forest, but the boat
heaved again, wiping the vision of trees from her thoughts and the
smile from her face.

*It feels like a lifetime since I was last here. So much has changed
in just a few months.*

It had been only two moons since the woman scouts had
accompanied her up to the mountain peaks and watched her cross
through the hidden rocky pass and descend to the opposite side,
where lay the newly discovered lands that previously had existed
for her clan, the Womara, only in myth.

Her fellow scouts had not been privy to all the aspects of her
journey to this new territory, nor to the prospect of her rendezvous with a prince named James. Before Seanna had begun her
descent from the peaks, she had thought, *If he comes, he could be
a king now.*

Seanna had saved James's life in these very mountains the
year before and had pledged to return to help retrieve the body
of his father, whom a band of assassins had murdered. She also
bore a heavy mandate from the newly formed alliance council, composed of a coalition of clansman from the surrounding
regions and led by Lord Arden, leader of the largest northern
township, to return with a proposed trade route with this new
realm, as a condition of the Womara's inclusion in the new
alliance.

She and the woman scouts had climbed the mountain trail
together from the Womara valley to the hidden pass. Seanna,
with Thea, her childhood friend and fellow warrior, at her side,

had stood at the crest in silence. Seanna had watched the amazed expressions on the women's faces as they viewed the wild vista before them for the first time.

The panorama extended for hundreds of miles of terrain, from the rocky slopes where they stood to a forest line in the distance. A glimpse of green valley touched the edges of a long, silver, winding river that snaked beyond their sight. Soft breezes blew around them, and the whisper of the winds made the hairs of Seanna's arms stand on end, as it had the first time she had beheld this expanse.

Thea placed her hand on her heart, her eyes welling with tears, and turned to Seanna. "I feel the presence of our ancestors here. I am beginning to understand why you have sought out the solace of these jagged peaks so many times. There is a spirit here that speaks to the soul."

"I am glad to share it with you," Seanna said.

The women stood in silence for a few more moments, before Seanna turned to her friends to say farewell.

"Why will you not take me with you?" Thea pleaded. "I will not have any peace until you return. We will face together, as warriors, whatever possible danger awaits you."

Seanna reached out and touched her hand gently. "I do not know what awaits me, but all my instincts tell me that I am not in danger. Do not fear, my friend. I go to fulfill my oath to the prince. I hope you can understand my reasons to go alone."

Seanna squeezed her friend's hand, then walked her horse forward. She turned back to her friends and smiled her encouragement. "I will see you here again in one moon," she said.

"Safe journey, and may the spirits of our ancestors protect you, Seanna," Thea called back.

Seanna nodded at Thea, who stood stoically with the other women at her side, then turned back to the desolate, rock-strewn slope and began her descent.

Ocean spray splashed over Seanna again, jolting her from her thoughts. As she pushed away the wet hair clinging to her face, she reflected, *So much has come to pass since I left my fellow warriors on the peaks. Where will I begin my tale of adventure and my reunion with James? Do I share that my heart has been forever changed, or will my newfound love show on my face?*

Seanna had already overstayed the length of her journey to the lands beyond the mountain pass, which her mother, Dian, the leader of the Womara, had decreed. Seanna had been comforted to know that a special messenger to her homeland, carrying a scroll bearing the seal of a king, had conveyed the news of her delayed return. The message bore the words of her well-being and her impending arrival in the next several weeks. For the moment, it was enough for her people to know that she was safe.

She was returning by sea, escorted by a personal envoy of the king's council, Lord Orman. Orman carried the king's pledge to meet with the alliance council and its leader, Lord Arden, to begin talks of the viability of trade between the two realms. An entourage of the king's surveyors and mappers accompanied them to chart their course.

Before her departure from James's court, Seanna had stood before his council in a formal ceremony to present the trade documents. James, in all his pomp, had handed her the parchments that contained words of introduction to the alliance and overtures of the proposed agreements between their regions. Lord Orman had the king's authority to execute those documents on behalf of James's realm.

In private, James had shared with Seanna his directive of any preliminary talks: that the Womara be included in the alliance council. It was a gesture he wished for Lord Orman to fulfill in exchange for the debt of gratitude James owed Seanna for having saved his life.

Seanna had expressed her concerns privately to James, and he had noted her cautionary words that the alliance would not welcome any implied contingencies, such as the Womara's inclusion in the council, to begin any talks.

"No one embarking on a negotiation wants a precondition to begin the discussion," James had acknowledged. "But Lord Orman is diplomatic and would not use any overture to force a position. I cannot fathom that the alliance will not recognize the value of what you have brought before them and see that you have secured this opportunity on your own merit."

Seanna's frown had betrayed her inner thoughts: *It is unfortunate that it must be Lord Orman who serves as envoy, as my sentiments regarding his nature have not changed. The king's council may have great faith in his abilities, but I still do not trust him.*

James had reached out to hold her hands in his. "It is of great consequence that you are the one who has earned this honor for the new alliance. Do not question your hard-earned respect."

Seanna had acquiesced, knowing in her heart that his words were true. So she had stood proudly before the king's council, knowing that she had gained an invaluable foothold in a new region and a strong prospect of trade between her clan and the people of the alliance.

Seanna wrapped her cloak around herself more tightly to

block the chill wind, but she warmed at the remembrance of James's smile when he handed her the documents.

My pride swelled, but I recognized that there is much work ahead to ensure that all will share in this new prosperity. My deepest hope is that the alliance council will honor the Womara's valuable role in securing this opportunity and our willingness to work toward a common goal.

The boat bucked, and Seanna gripped the rail again as the force of the wind rocked her off balance. The sight of Lord Orman climbing the stairs from the lower deck reminded her anew of the duties that lay ahead.

Lord Orman does not condone my union with his king, or our love. I care not. But I understand my role as the unpledged envoy for the Womara and will act accordingly.

She glanced in his direction as he leaned into the wind, struggling to keep himself upright as he made his way to the bow.

I have kept nothing of what I feel about this man secret from James, yet I have not been able to give him definitive evidence to support my suspicions.

In the days ahead, she would need to return to stand before Lord Arden and the alliance again, and set aside her residue of ill will regarding the Womara not gaining acceptance to the alliance council. She would also still face the divisiveness of Lord Warin, the clan lord of the largest southern realm, and whose open opposition to the Womara had influenced the council's vote. But she was ready for the challenge, and her spirit felt renewed when she thought of James's face shining with pride the morning of his ceremony when he presented the trade documents.

None of James's accolades about what opportunities I am bringing to the alliance can begin to measure the gift that he has given me. King or no king, treaties or not, he has my heart, and I have won his in return.

She hugged her arms tightly around herself, warding off the ache in her chest as she remembered James standing at his port's dock, bravely waving her off on her journey home. *I was torn because I missed my home, but I long for him already.* She placed her palm over her heart, her body tingling at the thought of his hand upon her breast.

Never in my wildest imaginings would I have thought that I would yearn with my whole being for any one man. Not a moment of the day passes when he is not in my thoughts.

In the early weeks of their new union, Seanna had found that she was not prepared for the onslaught of emotion and the abandonment of reason that each passing day brought as she found herself falling ever more in love with James.

She had been present at many of James's council meetings, which included discussions of the future of their regions. While she struggled to balance her sense of duty with the romantic abandon she felt around James, she admired him for his capacity to keep his thoughts focused on the daily duties of being king. His decisions and directives were for the good of his people, and she had witnessed what a fair and just leader he would be. *My respect for him deepened every day, and I knew I was in love with an honorable man.*

During brief lulls in the council discussions, James had stared across the room at her, making her stomach flutter, and she had had to catch her breath whenever he drew near. His eyes telegraphed a glint of mischief and a message that later, outside the formality of the meetings and behind the closed doors of his chamber, there would be no need for restraint. *Who could concentrate under such circumstances?* she wondered now, smiling to herself.

Their growing physical intimacy had deepened her wonder, and when their passions were satiated for the moment, they lay in each other's arms, sharing their thoughts—until a single caress of the skin or a lingering look inflamed their desire again. That thunderous, unbridled hunger had been unimaginable to her before James, yet she had surrendered to it willingly.

In their private time, she watched him for hours as he sat quietly and read, loving the way a lock of dark hair fell across his brow as he bowed his head in concentration. She would abandon her book to rise and place her arms around him from behind, hugging him close to inhale his scent deeply. She felt as if they were two animals drawn to each other, free to abandon themselves behind the closed doors of James's chamber, away from the prying eyes of the outside world.

Still, she struggled to gain control over the emotions that consumed her. *Have I lost myself? Am I not still a Womara and the same warrior?*

At times, she rebelled against the torrent of feelings and insisted to James that she ride alone for an hour or two. James nodded when she announced her intentions, intuitively understanding her need for the solitude and the quiet that fed her soul.

Once free of the castle walls, she spurred her horse to a full gallop and, riding hard, could connect with an old and familiar piece of herself, only to find that she could not elude the deception that nothing had changed. She traveled to the end of a length of invisible cord that now existed between her and James, and drew her back when the physical separation made her uncomfortable.

Her emotions exhausted from the ride, she returned with cheeks flushed not from the cool morning air, but from her musings about her lovemaking with James. Cedmon, the king's man, always waited in the stables for her, to report her safe arrival to James. "How was your ride today, Lady Seanna?" he always asked.

"Very pleasant" was her mumbled reply. As she saw her words bring a slight smile to his lips, she felt her cheeks grow redder and hoped he could not read her thoughts.

Returning to James's chamber, she was always greeted with a loving smile as she rushed into his waiting arms.

2

THE OLD FOX

Lord Orman struggled against the storm's wind as he attempted to climb the stairs to the upper deck of the boat. He saw Seanna standing at the bow, her long blond hair unbraided and blowing wildly in the wind. With deep green eyes that mirrored the intensity of the storm, she had turned to watch him grapple with his ascent.

She kept her gaze upon him, and he turned to meet it while bracing himself against the gusts that kept him slightly off balance. As he expected, she did not avert her eyes from his. *You always watch me like a hawk, Seanna*, he thought. He clenched his jaw, suppressing his annoyance at her overt act of viewing him unswervingly and with a look that he felt conveyed defiance.

I admit that your boldness still greatly disturbs me, especially my inability to judge the expressions and the emotions that lie beneath that fixed countenance. But I will not wither under the scrutiny of your gaze, Seanna, as a lesser man might. He bowed his head to her in a feigned gesture of congeniality that disguised his true thoughts.

Seanna responded in kind, before moving away from the bow with a small, shaky step. Orman turned to view the sea, noting the slight trace of salt upon his tongue. *I would rather stand against the wrath of the ocean's waves than be enclosed within the confining walls of my room belowdecks any longer.*

But he could still see Seanna in his peripheral vision. *You are indeed a worthy opponent, Seanna, and I know that you do not trust me. That is wise on your part. Because for me, there is no greater game than that of power, and you will never begin to understand the depth of my conviction.*

He smiled smugly to himself. *I possess the discipline to achieve my objectives, no matter how long it takes, and it is this element of discipline, coupled with restraint, that I consider one of my best attributes. Great men of ambition have been called upon to rise above the sheep and lead, but I have been content to know that my destiny lies in the shadow behind that man, propelling him on as I wait to gather the spoils of the aftermath.*

Orman turned from the dark horizon, glancing over his shoulder at Seanna, who was now standing by the captain and deep in conversation with him.

This fledgling alliance could offer so much for a man of my abilities, including an opportunity to emerge from the shadows that have always kept me hidden. If not for you, Seanna, and what you suspect of me, I might be assured an easy assimilation into this unseasoned gathering of men.

The loud laugh of the captain at something Seanna said broke through the sound of the blowing wind.

She is *charming when necessary,* Orman thought. As he watched her, he had to acknowledge how much she had changed in the short time that he had known her. *She adapts quickly and grows more confident in the role of leadership while blossoming under the love of the king.*

Still, he wondered if her newfound self-assurance, bolstered in part by the support of the king, would falter if it were challenged in front of the alliance. *We will see how you fare in the presence of your peers, and whether those emotions so tightly contained just beneath your perfectly controlled features will crack.*

He had garnered a reaction from her when he had suggested that James marry into a union that would solidify the kingdom, but he did not want to admit his failure in having not acted swiftly once he detected her vulnerability about her feelings for the king. Orman's opportunity to thwart the consummation of their love after the funeral of James's father, and in the last remaining days as Seanna had made her plans to leave, had been lost.

I failed again to drive a wedge between them while their love was still undeclared. I was close to watching her return to her homeland unfulfilled. I could have exacted my revenge for the humiliating defeat of Malcolm, the king's guard in the arena, where I thought her fighting skills would be defeated. Instead, I forfeited the king's confidence and drove Seanna into his arms.

The rocking boat made Orman's stomach feel the same way he had the day he had learned of James and Seanna's hasty departure, with a few of the king's closest guards, to the countryside. He had not held back his rage when Malcolm had informed him about it.

"Where have they gone?" Orman ranted.

"I do not know, thanks to you, in part, for I have lost a place of authority among the king's guard," Malcolm retorted.

"Be quiet, and do not forget your place," Orman snapped.

He feared the worst when he learned that the king had taken Seanna to his sanctuary, the forest cottage of his youth. Orman sensed that his battle to estrange them was lost when they returned several days later and his suspicions were confirmed: Seanna and James had changed. The transformation radiated from both of them; anyone in their presence could see it.

Orman remembered Seanna's face upon her return: The formerly hard edge of her features had softened and given her the glow of a woman in love. James was altered as well: he had the appearance of a man liberated from the weight of grief that he had carried over the past several years. The deep crease of his brow, a visual testament to the burden of his thoughts, had lessened, and a joyful smile illuminated his countenance. Two became one, and they made for a powerful union.

Orman shook his head at the remembrance. *It was my naive hope that the affair was just an infatuation born of the extraordinary circumstances of their encounter. I thought that James would soon tire of the conquest. But I misjudged the mold of his character, forged by his father and weaved together with strong moral fiber. He is the type of man who could find completeness in the love of one woman.*

"And that will be your downfall," Orman said into the wind.

When Seanna left the captain's company and descended the stairs to the lower deck, Orman approached him on the lookout landing and said, "I hope you have good news, that we will soon be out of these damn winds."

The captain laughed. "This is but a robust bluster. I have ridden the back of a far worse, bucking sea monster!"

Orman cringed at the dramatics. "When do we arrive, man?" he snapped.

The captain sobered. "As I told the lady, the storm does not impede our progress; it only drives us faster to our destination. It will break soon, and I would wager that we shall see land by tomorrow."

"We will see," Orman spat, dismissing the captain. He turned back to the indistinct horizon, still unwilling to go belowdecks, where the motion would surely cause him to vomit.

I can think with a clear head up here in the fresh air. My first step is arrival at the port of Lord Edmond, and then I'll be on to the court of Lord Arden and the alliance council, where, according to my spies, I may find dissent, and where my real work will begin.

A burst of pelting rain made him curse under his breath.

The sight of land cannot come soon enough. All my aspirations depend upon our surviving this bloody storm!

The storm broke in the night, as the captain had predicted, and Orman climbed the stairs in the morning to emerge on deck under a brilliant blue sky filled with fluffy white clouds with rays of light streaming through their openings. At the bow stood Seanna, one hand shading her eyes, gazing out toward the horizon. Following her sight line, he saw in the distance the thin contour of brown coastline that was her homeland. He joined her at the bow, standing beside her.

"Good morning, Lord Orman," Seanna said cheerily.

"It is indeed," he responded, "and is it not a relief to be past the unsettling motion of that storm?"

Seanna nodded but kept her eyes on the horizon as Orman leaned closer to her. "You must be very pleased to see your home again, Seanna."

She stepped back to look at him fully. "Yes, I am," she replied.

"Will your people be here to greet you?"

"I do not know," she answered.

"I look forward to meeting them, and I hope that your mother will be present. It will be disappointing if she is not." He smiled.

Seanna narrowed her eyes at his words, but she did not respond.

"There is so much to share. Will there be an announcement of an impending marriage?" Orman pressed.

Seanna's brow ceased with annoyance, and she gave him a constrained smile. "You know very well that there is to be no such thing, Lord Orman."

"Oh! Forgive my suggestion. I only assumed that such a declaration of a union would be an advantageous position for you with the alliance," Orman answered quickly.

"I will not discuss it with the alliance! In fact, you have made perfectly known to me your thoughts about the king's marriage prospects," Seanna snapped.

Orman shrugged. "Those were different days, and I can see that now. I am an old man conscripted to the old ways. But my king has a progressive mind that does not seem bound by convention or tradition."

Seanna squinted at him again. "Perhaps he sees the greater value of alliances between realms, not an empty, loveless bed with someone he is forced to marry out of protocol."

Orman nodded. "Ah, yes, he does have a greater aspiration to follow the calling of the heart and is fortunate to have found an ally in you." He paused, flashing his most accommodating smile, and watched Seanna's expression darken in response.

"If you'll excuse me, my lord, I must go below to prepare for our arrival."

Orman bowed low. "Of course," he replied, and returned to watch the thin line of the land grow larger in the distance as he rubbed warmth into his hands. He shielded his eyes against the sun and felt an unfamiliar tug at his heart. *This is a new place for me, a new beginning. But I feel a strange longing. What would it be like just to disappear into this unknown land, with no destination or objectives—simply to vanish into obscurity?*

Orman rubbed his forehead. *I must be weary from this journey. I am not the young man I once was.* The thought—*Not the young man I once was*—struck him hard, even as he tried to shake off the emotion. *Why my hesitation to proceed down this new path and complete what I have started? Do I grow burdened by conscience and falter at the thought of the lives that could be forfeited as I press relentlessly onward?*

His thoughts made his body tremble with chill, even in the warm morning air, as his heart winced at memories of the actions of his past. *Whatever has become of the young street urchin that I was? Why have I struggled to block his memory, when all that I did brought me here, to the pinnacle of my ambition?*

Orman inhaled the brisk sea air deeply to clear his thoughts. *But the dark memories always flood back. And no matter how hard I may try to stifle them, I am still that dirty, starving boy of the streets—until the day my life changed . . .*

3

THE STORY OF ORMAN

"Look out below!" a masonry worker yelled as Orman felt the first, thunderous jolt of the boulder, loosened from above the stone walls, as it hit the ramparts on the city's docks. After bouncing several feet into the air, it continued its trajectory toward the ground. Directly in its path stood the king and several guards, inspecting a newly constructed wall. They stood frozen, staring at the massive tumbling rock careening toward them.

Orman leaped from his place at the begging wall and knocked the king out of the path of the projectile as it landed with a massive thud in the spot where he had just stood. The guards rushed to their fallen monarch and roughly dragged Orman from the king's prone body.

"Your Grace, I am sorry . . . I meant only to . . . ," Orman stammered, before the guard holding him silenced him with a firm clap on the head.

"Stop," the king ordered, allowing the guards to help him up. "Leave him alone," he snapped, wiping the dirt and straw from his clothing and regaining his composure.

"Come here, boy," the king commanded, and Orman jumped up to step before him. "You are quick on your feet, aren't you, lad? What is your name?"

"I have no real name, Your Grace," Orman lied. He had had one long ago, but ever since he was a small child he had answered to Rag Boy, because he had grown up in the local laundry house.

"No name?" the king questioned.

"None of importance, Your Grace," Orman answered. "I have no parents and have known only the streets for as long as I can remember," he lied again. "There are no names out here."

The king looked at him intently as Orman shifted his stance slightly under the scrutiny. He looked down at his ragged garments. *How filthy I must look. He must be horrified that I touched him!*

"This is where you have always lived?" the king asked.

"Yes, Your Grace," Orman answered, looking away from the king's gaze, careful not to betray his untruth while simultaneously justifying to himself that some of his words were in fact based in fragments of veracity.

It was true that he had never known his parents. He was the bastard child of some unknown whore from a nearby brothel, left on the doorstep of the local laundry. Had someone abandoned him there because it was known that one of the young laundresses had just lost her child? *Was I loved for even a brief moment? Did whoever left me hope that the young woman's grieving heart would compel her to take in a defenseless foundling?*

The instincts of his wretched mother, whoever she was, had been right. The young laundress had coveted the small and helpless bundle as a gift from God to replace her dead child. She had no home and lived in the laundry quarters, in exchange for part of her wages, after her lover had abandoned her when he learned she was with child.

The distraught woman assured the proprietor that the child would not hinder her work, and, after much persuading, she was permitted to keep him in the laundry quarters. The mother and child lived together in the interior of that miserable place. His cradle consisted of dirty sheets waiting to be washed; he was moved from pile to pile during the day. At night, they both slept upon a makeshift bed of abandoned sheets.

Orman had known only the love of his adopted mother, and he often speculated that her affection in those early years must have saved him from utter emotional detachment. The lung disease that plagued most laundresses after years of harsh soaps, confined quarters, and putrid air had taken her life. He had watched her die, gasping and coughing up blood, yet Orman had difficulty recounting his feelings of loss at the time; he had only a vague memory of fear from when the dark-clothed men came to take her body away on a wooden cart.

The busy laundry was no place for the young child, and his protection ended with the death of his foster mother. At six years of age, he was turned out onto the streets, and the warmth and affection of her embrace were quickly forgotten as he began a daily struggle to survive.

Those early years on the streets were hard, but he grew into a youth of ten years. He scavenged and stole, learning to tell a lie with a fixed expression if it gained him what he needed. His instincts were honed by his daily begging encounters, and he intuitively learned when to play with people's emotions.

He staked a place at the city's wall to beg by beating back other street urchins' challenges of his claim. He was at the wall at the same time of day when most townsfolk made their way back home from their morning shopping in the market. They carried baskets full of the day's meals, and he pleaded with them for a tossed apple or vegetable. At night, he visited taverns and dark alleys to sell a different set of wares and earn a meal for the day.

Standing before the king now, Orman would never tell him that he had been nicknamed for the pile of rags he slept on. On the streets, he had no friends and no need for any name. But he quickly brightened with an idea.

"It would please me if you gave me a name, Your Grace," he chirped, "so that I may always remember this day."

The king laughed out loud, and the guards grinned. "So be it. I will name you Orman. It means Brave One. Your heroic act today has changed the course of your life, young man."

"Bring him," the king commanded his guards.

That fateful day had indeed changed his life, Orman thought, for the king had been true to his word. Orman's circumstances had changed dramatically over the next several years. He was given a job within the castle's kitchen, fetching and cleaning for the cooks. In the evenings, exhausted, but with a full stomach, he dropped onto his straw bed in his corner of the kitchen pantry, and a small smile crossed his face as he contemplated his good fortune before he fell into a deep sleep.

I had a place to sleep that was safe, warm, and dry, and a solid meal every day. I whispered a silent vow each night that I would work hard, because I was determined to keep my place in the castle and never return to the streets again.

Orman endeavored to keep himself at every opportunity in the sight of the king, who checked on his progress on occasion. Orman was a resourceful youth, and in time his position was elevated to that of page. That gave him freedom to roam the palace, observing every aspect of the working castle and much about its inhabitants.

One day, the king caught him eavesdropping outside the library, where several young sons of the court's nobles received tutored instruction.

"What it is that you are listening to, Orman?" the king asked.

"The teacher speaks of faraway places that I never imagined existed, and of languages unknown to me. Have you seen these places, Your Grace?"

"I have seen some," the king answered, smiling, "and they can be wondrous. You are welcome to take from the library any book that you wish to read for yourself," he offered.

Orman felt himself flush. "I am ashamed to say that I cannot read."

The king placed his hand on Orman's shoulder. "Of course—how remiss I am to think that you might. We will change that."

The next day, Orman was assigned a tutor to instruct him in reading and writing, and was thereupon awakened to a world of literature, poetry, philosophy, and history. The acquisition of knowledge consumed him, and he spent his extra hours reading well into the night by candlelight. He was soon allowed to sit with the young lords of the castle, having attained their learning level, and ultimately became the best student among them.

But Orman's fellow students taunted him behind the back of the teacher, spilling his ink upon his writing or hiding his quills. They called him low-born, and he often sat alone, excluded from their games. He told himself that he did not care, justifying the calculating coldness underlying his feeling and silently mocking their stupidity.

I will show you all! For my ambition will far exceed all your feeble aspirations.

Fate had given him a rare chance to change his destiny, but he understood that he must be the one to capitalize on such good fortune. His street upbringing had made him savvy in the ways to exploit a man's weakness, and living in the king's court gave him the opportunity to hone those abilities. He rose quickly among the ranks of the nobles and, as a young man of the court, continued to make himself invaluable to the king. He acted with false airs but knew deep down he was easily one step away from the gutter from which he had been rescued. Orman respected the king's authority but could not help but question the soft heart of a man who would take a boy like him into his home.

The birth of the king's first son and future heir to the throne, James, gave Orman the focused objective of building a deeper relationship with the king by making himself a resource in the young prince's daily life. He earned the honor of overseeing the prince's education and, later, that of James's young cousin Thomas, who joined the household after his father died.

Orman lacked a noble pedigree and its accompanying wealth and influence, but a solution was within reach if he had the opportunity to marry into a high-born household. He set his eye upon a suitable young daughter of a prominent noble of the court, though she was to be merely an innocent pawn for his aspirations.

He continued to cultivate the king's confidence, feigning frustration at lacking the attributes that would have made him worthy of such a marriage. As he had hoped, the king intervened on his behalf by offering his blessing. Orman had chosen wisely, and the marriage elevated his status in court. His bride was a young beauty, and the prominence of her family made him the envy of many men.

I remember the first time I lifted your wedding veil and looked upon you as my wife, he recalled. *As you stood with your head bowed demurely before me, so hopeful, I knew I would never love you and that you would be just a piece in the mosaic of my ambition.*

In truth, he detested women. He could not fathom their value beyond their obvious role in bearing children and satisfying men's carnal desires. He could never love a woman. *I desire men. I always have.*

His attraction to his own sex was the reason he had never found working in back alleys as disgusting as had the other street boys who sold themselves for a penny to the nobles who frequented those haunts. And he relished the feeling of power he held, knowing those men's shadowy secrets.

Strange, though, that I have not thought of my wife in years, he mused. *Once she served her purpose as the stepping-stone to my wealth, I wiped her from my thoughts.*

He had performed his spousal duties well enough to get her with child, but he had no desire to be a husband or a father. She would never bring her child to term, and both mother and unborn son had died unexpectedly, of a cause known only to Orman: he had induced death by dropping a small amount of poison into her wine, forcing her into early labor and then a coma from which she never recovered.

Orman had spent a brief period of his youth as a courier in the local apothecary, where he had become familiar with basic herbs. The shelves of the cramped and dimly lit store were lined with jars that contained bat wings, dried flowers, toads floating in jars of green liquid, exotic herbs, and many other things he did not care to know about. He wandered the shop, enjoying the smell of incense as he watched the proprietor grind a certain herb or flower into powder or drip an extract into a small bottle. He had ultimately gained a basic understanding of many herbs that would prove invaluable in the years to come and that, when applied in the correct dosage, could be used as poisons.

Upon the unfortunate death of his young wife, Orman retained her wealth and title and convincingly played a grieving widower, vowing never to marry again in honor of her memory. His wife would not be the first to lose her life to serve his ambitions or vices. *How many have I sacrificed to this relentless drive for more power? I can no longer count them.*

At times, an overly ardent lover had required silencing. Orman would never expose his aberrations by frequenting the dark alleys of his youth but instead sexually seduced young pages or manservants of the visiting nobles, using his influence to promise them advances in their station and threatening them into secrecy when they pressed him to fulfill his promises. He kept his clandestine life well hidden at any cost, including stilling loose tongues, if necessary, and never tarnished the illusion of his dedication to his king and the young princes.

The king and Orman's relationship deepened more and more over the years. They often walked the grounds of the castle, engaged in conversation, or sat for hours in the library, puzzling over a game of chess. The king appreciated that Orman had a talent for military thinking and relished political discourse, which made him an engaging confidant. In time, the king sought him out frequently to discuss current politics.

I knew I had achieved the pinnacle of my career when I was appointed a lord and given a seat on the king's advisory council. But why was that not enough?

Orman shifted in discomfort at the question, for he knew the answer. His chest tightened at the dark memory of the king's assassination, which Orman himself had been instrumental in contriving.

For your act of generosity and kindness so long ago, I betrayed you, my king. The first day I crossed your path ultimately cost you your life. When I understood the depth of my quest for power, a plan formed. I had to plot your death and that of your heir, James, in order to place Thomas upon the throne.

My ambition requires a younger, more malleable prince, one who will enable me to yield greater influence and direct his actions from the shadows. Thomas will be a puppet king, and I will be the one pulling the strings.

4

LOVE AND SHADOW

James stood at the edge of the docks, watching the sails of Seanna's boat recede on the horizon until it disappeared from his sight. He turned to Cedmon with a stricken face and asked, "How could I have let her go?" He shook his head and rubbed his forehead as he scanned the empty vista.

"She needed to return to her home, if only for a brief time, Your Grace," Cedmon answered.

James nodded back weakly. "But it is a challenging time to be in love and at the same time on the brink of new beginnings, combined with an unclear future."

"I understand your feelings, Your Grace. These *are* uncertain times, especially in light of the new information that your spies have revealed about those who have given your cousin sanctuary."

James nodded. "Thomas has found an ally in the barbarian king Halvor, ruler of a small continent to the far north and across the great sea. These barbarians are feared raiders, known for their conquests of surrounding lands and vulnerable townships along coastlines. I can only imagine what Thomas has offered to secure this king's support and the army of rabble behind him."

"He has offered a kingdom, I imagine," Cedmon answered.

"Indeed. Yet my council believes that I have been beating a premature drum about the need to prepare for conflict," James answered. "This new information should change their position."

"I think so," Cedmon said.

"I never shared my instincts with anyone, even my father, about what I sensed in my cousin's increasingly dark moods and growing menace. He was always one to pursue his own frivolity, but he changed into a sullen and angry young man. I did not bother to seek out the cause of his malcontent and sought only to avoid his black humor. How could I have imagined that his dark turn would take shape in the evil act of plotting my father's death?"

Cedmon furrowed his brow. "You could not have known the deepest recesses of your cousin's mind or the extent of his treachery. He withdrew into himself."

James nodded. "After the assassination of my father, the council declared that if Thomas were ever captured, he would be condemned to death as the mastermind behind the plot. But my spies have returned with news that supports my greatest fear: that he attempts to gather an army against me."

Cedmon said, "You were prudent to call for the reaffirmation of our alliances with neighboring regions and to solidify our borders with their leaders, as your suspicions may come to fruition." He paused, then added, "Does Lady Seanna know of the news from your spies, Your Grace?"

"Yes, she did, but I did not want her concerns for me to taint her return home as she prepared herself to stand before her new alliance council."

"Surely, they will view your proposal to trade with Seanna's southern continent as a valuable strategy for our region," Cedmon said. "And it cannot harm your position of defense."

"A trade union is all that she and I discussed. We are just beginning our discourses with the alliance, and I would not want these talks to be compromised over speculations of a looming threat from my cousin."

"Does anyone beyond our council, Lord Orman, and Seanna know of Thomas' new alliance with the King Havlor?" Cedmon asked.

"No, and that information is not a strong basis on which to begin any negotiations with the new alliance," James added.

"Let us hope that Lord Orman will temper this knowledge in service of everyone's best interests," Cedmon replied.

James smiled weakly, placing his hand upon his man's shoulder. "In spite of the timeliness of these talks, I still feel selfish for not wanting Seanna to go, or for wishing I were with her. These will be long and lonely days without her company."

"It will be a short time before you will be reunited again, and think what a homecoming it will be, Your Grace."

James tensed his jaw as he looked out to the sea again. "Those are happy thoughts, but now, in her absence, I will move in earnest to secure renewed pledges from the lords of our surrounding regions."

"I know that some of the preliminary talks have vexed you," Cedmon said.

"Yes, I was often preoccupied with those discussions, and I spent more time than I desired venting my sentiments to Seanna."

"Lady Seanna understands your challenges," Cedmon offered.

James nodded. "I am blessed to have won the heart of a tolerant woman, and a warrior, no less."

"She realizes the threat of your cousin's treachery. Her clan has fought fiercely to maintain their independence. A pact with her region could be welcome and necessary for you, even if you do not ask it of her," Cedmon added.

"Yes, but that pledge of alliance is not hers to give," James reminded him. "She travels home with Lord Orman to begin diplomatic talks and secure her clan's future first." He paused, then added, "I admire her dedication to her clan and their progress. My council cautioned me not to hope for too much from the outcome of these preliminary talks, given that Seanna is an inexperienced and unacknowledged emissary, but I did not accept all of their forecasting."

"I can understand some of their cautions, but Lord Orman does not carry my wholehearted support in negotiating on her behalf," Cedmon said.

"Nor mine, but it was not the right time to oppose the council and create dissent. I did declare privately to Orman my condition that the Womara be included at the table of the alliance council before any discussions."

A seagull squawked overhead, and James looked upward to follow its flight. He turned back to Cedmon and said, "No more talk of dissent today. All this speculation only adds to my heavy heart after Seanna's departure. I want some time alone, to return to the musings of a young man in love."

"Of course, Your Grace," Cedmon said.

As he and Cedmon rode back from the docks, James's thoughts wandered to the events of the past month. Upon returning with

Seanna from his boyhood home and having won her love, he had been appeased by the knowledge that she would remain with him for the time being, and had pushed aside the darkening cloud of his cousin's treachery that now compelled him to action.

He had delayed summoning the lords of the regions to debate the possible threats from Thomas. After his father's funeral, he had listened to the older lords' many expressions of condolence, followed by whispered cautionary words not to place too much stock in the cowardly actions of a weak cousin.

Many of the leaders were skeptical of Thomas's ability to cultivate a grand design of foreign alliance from anyone who must have given him sanctuary. The Thomas everyone thought they knew had no temperament to mastermind a real challenge against the crown. When had he ever displayed such ambition? the lords argued. They advised James to exercise restraint following the dark days after his father's death, and to temper any hasty action born of his inexperience as a new king. But for James, their words rang hollow.

Here I stand, having just buried my father, and these men ask for caution? The king lies cold within his tomb, a poignant reminder to me that treachery and death are always close. Let my instincts be my guidance now, and I will never allow myself that vulnerability of blind trust again.

Sometimes, alone with his own judgment, he felt himself waver: *Do I blame the lords and the king's council for lacking confidence in me because I am a new king and untested?* But when he stood before them, he summoned his courage and set aside his doubts, telling them, "My lords, you cannot wait for assurances that I will be able to lead. You must trust that I am my father's son."

He initiated an unprecedented move to build an additional council of advisors, composed of the most talented military minds within his ranks, and surrounded himself with the youngest and brightest sons of his most loyal lords.

In private counsel, Lord Orman extended his concerns that James should follow the direction of his advisors. "The council must send spies to confirm that Thomas is moving against you," Orman argued.

James snapped, "I will deal with the council, and you should concentrate on the duties that lie ahead as you prepare to depart with Seanna to the new realm. I hold you accountable for a favorable outcome in our overtures with the alliance council and its leader, Lord Arden."

In the days that followed, James had recalled several exasperated departures from the council chambers. During one such episode, as he stormed out with Cedmon at his side, he had said, "If I hear one more word about 'caution' and 'restraint' from those old goats, I will go mad."

Most times I can temper my words when conducting the business of the court, he had thought. *I try to be just as careful and practiced in my judgments before the council as I grow into my role as king.*

Cedmon had raised an eyebrow at James's outburst, as he rarely witnessed such demeaning words from his king, but had also offered encouragement. "The council offers caution as they have seen men turn self-indulgent and cruel when they possess the power of dominion over others' lives. I do not fear that of you, my king—stay your course. Gaining the council's confidence will require patience. Many of the older council members are slow to change their thoughts."

"I was wrong to call them old goats," James said, "but they vex me."

Cedmon nodded. "At times they will, but have they not earned a degree of respect for the years of counsel they provided to your father and now are providing to you?"

James stopped and turned to Cedmon. "I think my father would approve of my progressive thinking. I feel his presence, and he guides me when he speaks to me in my quiet moments. His words tell me that this is not the time for careful measures and that I must be bold in my actions."

"You must listen to that voice, then, and believe that your father's spirit is with you," Cedmon answered. "I, too, believe in omens and the whispers of dreams. I confess that when a soft breeze lightly touches my cheek, I choose to believe it is the presence of my deceased wife."

James nodded. "I feel there will always be a strong bond between my father and me—one that even death cannot separate." He felt a lump rise in his throat and looked away for a moment. "But it is my compassion for the less fortunate that bears my mother's influence," he continued. "She did not tolerate self-indulgence or demeaning behavior toward the underprivileged."

"She was a wonderful woman," Cedmon acknowledged.

Yes, James thought, *but that influence cannot negate the treachery of betrayal. The murder of my father changed me forever, and I will never measure men's worth the same way I once did.*

Cedmon seemed to understand that Seanna was the exception to the king's restraint. James had shared his travails when she rescued him from the mountain but could not explain his blind trust in a woman who was a stranger.

"I cannot describe it, but even when her bow was drawn against me, I knew she would not harm me," James recounted.

"But she never told you much about herself in those early encounters," Cedmon said.

"She did not need to. I grew to trust her. I did not question much, and maybe that is why I survived."

"Yes, and I see that you and Lady Seanna have the same bond that your mother and father shared. I am happy for you."

"And what of your own heart, Cedmon? Was it how it was with your wife?" James asked.

"Yes, it was."

"And did you feel that your world changed with this love?"

"What do you mean, Your Grace?" Cedmon asked.

James was quiet for a moment. "It is that I have newfound fears. . . . I fear loss. What would I do without her love? If something happened to her, how would I live?"

"You simply would," Cedmon answered.

"I am beginning to understand where men find the strength to stand before the charge of battle, knowing that they fight for everything they love. I would not fear death if I fought to save her," James added.

"I hope that you never face that sacrifice, my king. Or need to draw upon your strength of will to issue commands that condemn men's lives with a call to battle. I have seen men change under the weight of such a burden and I wish you days of joy ahead," Cedmon stated solemnly.

When James had returned with Seanna from the forest to the camp of his men, Cedmon had been the first to greet him. "Your Grace," Cedmon had said. "How may we be of service?"

James knew he could not contain his joy. "Cedmon, it is a beautiful day, is it not?"

"It is indeed."

"Indeed." James slapped Cedmon's back, before announcing, "The lady and I shall stay in the forest for a while. Will you send a man back to announce that the king is enjoying his leisure and will return soon? Some food and wine will be most welcome."

Cedmon signaled for a manservant.

"All is well, Cedmon," James called out over his shoulder, as he turned to walk back into the forest.

"I am glad, my king. And Lady Seanna?"

"Most wondrous," James shouted back.

As James had taken one last look at his men, he had overheard Cedmon say, "Well, you heard the king's command. What are you waiting for?" Then James's man had turned away so that the others could not see his grinning face.

5

THE OWL CALLS

After returning to the castle grounds, James retired to the solitude of his chamber. He slumped in an armchair in the corner of his room, rubbing his temples and remembering the sight of Seanna's ship sailing away and the effort it had taken him to put on a brave face when she departed.

He ate his dinner alone in his room that night. After his meal, he lingered on his balcony, taking pleasure in the quiet of the evening and viewing the waxing moon in the night sky. The stones of the balcony wall felt rough to his touch as he leaned out to smell the fragrance of the blooms on the vine crawling up the trestle. The scent evoked a physical reminder of the first night that Seanna had stood beside him in this place, as they had stared out at the sky.

How timid I was, unable to tell you how beautiful you looked in the soft light of the ending day. Did I stare too long? Could you have heard the thumping of my heart if I had dared to step closer?

Breathing deeply, he filled his lungs with sweet air as he

watched the darkness descend and strained his ear to listen to the sounds of emerging nocturnal creatures. A rustle in the leaves below, of some small animal in the garden, brought to mind Seanna's attunement to the night. She had enhanced his awareness that even within the stone walls of his palace, he could find nature all around him when he listened with intention. He knew that the days ahead, filled with upcoming debates and strategies, would keep him occupied, but it was folly to think he could suppress his yearning for Seanna whenever he was alone, in silence.

As he stared at his empty bed, he thought, *How can I look upon this and wipe away the vision of you lying naked upon fur skins, my love, or the color of the firelight upon your skin, or your smile?*

He rubbed his chest to soothe the ache in it, when the distant hoot of an owl in a garden tree made him grin. *Have you sent your owl to comfort me, Seanna? Are you thinking of me, too, and of our first night?*

The owl called again from the trees, and another owl responded as James kept his hand upon his heart. *Ah, your call has been answered. You have found your mate, just as I have.*

James had never been in love before and did not know if most men were honest enough to admit the power that a woman could hold over them. As a younger man, prompted by the goading of his friends, he had limited his experiences with women to the local brothels. Those fumbling, brief, and lusty encounters contrasted sharply with the hunger for Seanna that now consumed him.

The insatiable desire he experienced defied reason as he sought to explore every facet of her physically, or when the act of her simply lying in his arms calmed him. The depth of Seanna's unbridled passion astonished him as well. She was free in the expression of her ardor, unconstrained by the social dictates that stifled the women of his culture. She loved him with her whole body and soul.

His loins stirred at the thought of her as he looked up again at the dark sky and the sliver of moon, recalling the first night they had made love, lying on a bed of ferns within the forest. The memory of Seanna's naked body bathed in the light of a full moon as they lay breathing deeply to quiet their beating hearts made him ache again. He had watched her face brighten as she listened to the sounds of the forest around them and the hoot of a distant owl echoing through the trees.

She smiled. "That is a good omen. Listen—let's see if another will answer back. They call to each other."

Within a few seconds, another owl answered with a hoot from deeper within the forest.

"So, the animals talk to you, too," James teased.

"The owl is my totem animal," Seanna answered.

"What does that mean?"

"It is the animal that guides me, and I seek wisdom from its presence. So, yes, they do speak to me."

James rolled to his side, grinning down at her.

"You are laughing at me?" Seanna asked, as she lifted herself on her elbow, cradling her head in her hand.

"No, my love," James answered, softly stroking her cheek. "I would not mock your nature gods."

"The owl can see in the dark and transfers its spirit to those under its protection, allowing them to see beyond what others perceive," she said.

"It is a gift, then?" James asked.

"Yes, in a way. What creature might be your totem?" Seanna asked.

"I do not know. I have never thought of an animal in that way—only in terms of the role that they play in the hunt."

"Is there no animal that merits your admiration? One that draws your observation, that you watch more than others?"

James intertwined his fingers with hers and drew her fingertips to his lips, kissing them lightly, considering her question.

"I love the beauty of the hawk in flight. I have wondered what it must be like to soar free above everything, and in my dreams, sometimes I fly."

"That is a spiritual awakening," Seanna said. "In your dreams, your animal appears to guide or warn you."

"These are the spirits of your forest?" James asked.

"Yes, and everything that surrounds them."

"I will watch and listen for mine," James said. "It will bring our worlds together." He reached for her again, and she jumped up, laughing, eluding his grasp.

"Come," she said. "I want to bathe in the river."

They walked together hand in hand to the edge of the moving water, and James watched from the bank as Seanna stepped in and submerged herself. When she rose, he caught his breath as the moonlight cast a blue glow on her naked skin and the rivulets of liquid trickling down between her breasts shone like silver.

He stood to offer his hand as she emerged. He drew her to him and led her to a shallow pool. He sat back in the water and pulled her onto his lap. Seanna smiled and mounted him willingly. James pulled her closer and with his tongue licked a water droplet from her skin. They rocked slowly together as Seanna arched her back and pressed harder against him. When she cried out softly, he could not hold back his own climax.

Satisfied for the moment, they lay beside the pool for a long time, letting the warm night air dry their bodies.

"Do these woods feel the same as yours?" James asked.

"Of course, some things are the same," she said. "My forest is mystical to me, infused with the spirits of my people. I hope that I can share its power with you soon."

"I want to see it more than anything," James answered. "To embrace your world is to know the essence of who you are, and that is very important to me."

Seanna smiled and kissed him softly.

"I wonder if my world can ever be home for you," he said, as she lightly stroked the edges of his face and ran her fingertips over his brow.

"Do not worry about such things. We do not have to answer all our questions now, do we? We have time to learn about each other."

James sighed deeply as he leaned toward her. "Yes, you are right. We do not need all the answers, but right now, I wish never to leave this place. Especially if I could keep you here forever, just as you are now, in this light," he mused.

"It is wonderful, is it not?" Seanna said, gazing at the trees surrounding them.

James nodded. "It is indeed. In fact, I am so bewitched that I do not quite feel myself." He leaned closer to her and whispered, "I am different. I feel like one who has lost himself. I cannot fully explain the sensation."

Seanna looked deep into his eyes. "I am lost, too. I have no comparison, for I have never given myself completely to another man. But in this moment, I know what my heart says."

"Do we speak of love?" James asked.

"I have already loved you for a long time," Seanna said, smiling.

James drew her even closer. "Kiss me again," he commanded.

The next morning, James awoke to light streaming through the cottage window and turned to gaze at Seanna's sleeping form beside him. He smiled lovingly as he reached out to touch her tousled hair, causing her to stir and roll over toward him.

"Good morning, my love," she said. She smiled as she sat up and stretched. "I was dreaming. For a moment I thought I might have conjured you and all that happened last night. I had a moment of fear that I would wake to find myself alone. But my dreams are true, for here you are." She leaned in to kiss him.

"Shall we relive your dreams?" James grinned as he reached for her.

Seanna moved quickly from the bed, laughing, eluding his embrace, and announcing, "I am starving." As she began to search through the remains of their food, she said, "We have little left; I may need to hunt for rabbits. Do your duties require that we return soon?"

"No," James answered. "I think not. I have imagined having you here for such a long time that I will not be so hasty to leave. I must inform Cedmon of our plans to stay longer; that way, we can also replenish our supplies."

"That would be wonderful," Seanna said.

James flashed her a longing look as she stopped her search through the cupboards and returned to the edge of the bed.

For the next few days, they stayed in his cottage while exploring the surrounding forest. They frequented a small waterfall that cascaded into a pool surrounded by moss-covered rocks, where they sat contentedly for hours, sharing more stories about their lives.

Seanna gathered wild foods, such as the unfurled leaves of ferns and wild mushrooms, and she knew the places in the still water where fish hid in the shadows of overgrown roots or a submerged log. She often caught them with her hands.

At sunset, they built a small fire and Seanna cooked what she had found, placing the cleaned fish with the greens and mushrooms, wrapped in large leaves, on the ebbing coals as they sat by the warmth of the flames, drinking wine and talking. When Seanna handled James his cooked bundle, he opened the charred leaves and began to eat the steamed contents with his hands.

He stopped midbite. "This is delicious," he exclaimed. "Not only are you a beautiful woman and a warrior, you cook as well."

"This is the extent of my cooking," Seanna said, chuckling. "My people are foragers, and we survived in the early days on what nature provided to us. We are blessed when the forest gives us our food."

"Even eating is an experience with you," James said between bites of his meal. "There is still so much I want to know about your people." He paused to pour her more wine.

"And I will tell you everything," she answered.

"In these quiet times together, I feel our worlds merging," James said. "Duties fall away, and it is just us. We know so little about each other, yet I still feel as if I have known you a lifetime."

"It is a strange thing to feel so comfortable," Seanna acknowledged.

"You must tell me more stories of your people's history, so that when I travel to your home, I will not be such a stranger."

Seanna smiled sadly at his words. "My people's lineage is not as long as yours; I can trace it back only a few generations. Earlier than that, we are a scattered people."

"It must be hard to have lost so much," James said.

Seanna nodded. "Yes, but we forged a new beginning on the day my ancestors escaped into the forest. My mother is Dian, and her mother was Landra. Landra was the daughter of Rowan, my great-great-grandmother who was killed during the invasion. I shared her story with you and your men when we first reunited in the mountains."

"It was a powerful tale of courage and sacrifice," James said.

Seanna picked a small flower from the grass and threw it into the flames. "And at our sacred fires, we always honor their memories."

James nodded. "Tell me more of them."

"We do carry the collective sadness of a people who began in slavery, and our hearts are heavy with the memories of people and places lost to us. My ancestors were forced to give up hope of ever returning home, so they built a new world. I was told the way my great-great-grandmother once described us: 'The women of the Womara are like seeds carried on the wind, not knowing their journey's end, but where they land, a beautiful flower grows.'"

"My kin lie entombed in our family crypt for many generations back, and it gives me solace to know that they are there," James said.

"I derive the same comfort from my own ancestors' passing," Seanna answered.

"How so?"

"Upon death, the Womara's bodies are returned to the sacred flames, and their ashes are scattered within the forest, nourishing the earth. Their spirits are renewed by giving life to the trees and plants. When I look up into the foliage in spring and see the sprouting buds on the branches, I think of my people and the gift of new life."

James looked at her for a long time, before continuing, "The way you speak of these things makes me view life in a different way. It is a beautiful sentiment to experience the renewal of nature as a reflection of your loved ones."

He took her hand. "You have shared the tale of the invasion of your homeland, and the great battle where you lost many women and your kin Rowan, but what became of the women who survived?"

Seanna took a drink of her wine. "I believe this is where the real story of the Womara begins. Rowan taught the women to fight against enslavement and how to survive, but it was her daughter, Landra, who rebuilt our devastated numbers after the battle and brought trade to our clan. My grandmother Landra was a visionary who molded our future. She was born into the Womara world and never questioned her equality or her right to be free. She lived that belief every day and manifested the prosperity that we continue to enjoy today.

"After the raiders' invasion and the battle we won against them, she secured the treaty to our lands that granted us a permanent home and a place of recognition among the clans. She understood the need to bring self-sufficiency to the Womara, and to progress. We advanced by learning the trades."

"There were not many women left at the end of the battle to rebuild your clan. How did they learn these skills?" James asked.

Seanna reached out and took his hand. "I am grateful that you are interested in my history. You remind me so much of Lord

Stuart. He asks many questions and is always ready for a good tale."

"Do you love this man?" James asked.

"I do love him," Seanna answered. "I served as his bodyguard when we were young. We have traveled a long path and together have faced down death. He is like a brother to me."

"That sounds like another story," James said.

"It is, but that is for another night. Tonight, let me speak of my grandmother, for her memory warms my heart. She lived to old age, and when she passed on her leadership to my mother, she had many hours to share tales with her inquisitive young grand-daughter. Her story will help you understand how the Womara became what we are."

6

THE DEAD RETURN

Landra stared across the battlefield at the dead and dying warriors as the morning mists encircled their bodies and mingled with their departing souls. Amid groans and cries for help from the wounded, she stood with Asha, her mother, Rowan's, closest friend and second in command of the Womara warriors, at her side. Lord Alfred, the young lord of the northern region, who had just saved the Womara from a final slaughter at the hands of invading barbarians, stood rigid with them.

Landra dropped to her knees and hunched over her mother's body, unable to pull herself away to tend to the living. *We were so close to being saved, Mother. Only a few moments more, and you might have lived!*

Lord Alfred extended his hand to touch her shoulder. "We will help you gather your dead and build their funeral pyres before we depart."

Landra felt her face flush as she looked up him. "I cannot leave her here." She glanced around wildly, and Asha came to her side, raising her gently to her feet.

"There is nothing more to do, Landra. We must prepare the dead."

Landra's body tensed under Asha's touch as she stood, never taking her eyes off her mother's still form.

"No. We cannot leave our people here in this place of death. We will take them home to our sacred fires. The purity of the flames will release their spirits to wander in peace among our forest."

Asha stared into her eyes and grasped her shoulders. "That will be a great undertaking, but if that is your wish, so be it."

Landra turned to face Lord Alfred. "You may not understand our ways, but we will be comforted that they are near us."

"Then allow us to help you make ready the dead," he answered.

Landra signaled to Asha. "Send a scout ahead," she ordered. "Announce our victory with the aid of Lord Alfred and his men. Tell our people that we return with the fallen and that they must prepare the pyres in the great meadow."

Landra stepped closer to the young lord standing before her and bowed her head, hand on her heart. "I am blinded in my grief, Lord Alfred, and remiss in not expressing my gratitude for your having answered the warning call. I am indebted. If not for you and your men, all would have been lost."

"No words are needed," Alfred replied. "Your mother's quick action in meeting the raiders, and the sacrifice of your warriors, saved many more lives."

Landra glanced back at Rowan's body. "Let us make camp and treat our wounded. Many of these women are healers."

Landra walked among the strewn corpses, closing the open eyes of the dead and bowing her head in silent grief, refusing food until she had checked every fallen Womara. Their bodies were moved gently, and whenever a wounded woman was found alive, the healers rushed to her aid, but any unfortunate raider still struggling for breath was quickly put to death. Landra returned to Asha's side to keep vigil beside her mother.

"I watched you in the distance, moving among the fallen," Asha said. "You have already assumed the role of leader and will carry on your mother's legacy. She would be so proud."

Landra's throat tightened, and her head sagged. "We have survived the battle, but we have lost so many!"

Asha nodded and dropped to her knees beside Landra. Reaching out to grasp her hand, she spoke softly: "You must be strong now." She looked down at Rowan and spoke to her pale form, "Your daughter will make a fine leader, because she is like you." She smiled at Landra, her eyes brimming with tears.

Landra studied her mother's face. *You look so peaceful, Mother.* Rowan's creased brow had softened in death's repose; only a small drop of blood at the corner of her mouth betrayed that something was wrong and that she was not merely in a deep sleep.

Asha brushed the hair back from Rowan's waxen face and turned to Landra again. "I remember the day you were born. Your mother paced that whole morning, cursing with the pain of birth. When the time drew near, she squatted and held the birthing pole, panting like a wild animal. When you slid from her body, I caught you, wiping you free of afterbirth and cutting your umbilical cord.

"'What did I have?' your mother implored.

"'She is a girl!' I proclaimed, as I lifted you high in my hands above our heads, welcoming you to life with the cry of our people, before placing you in Rowan's arms. She glowed with such pride and love, and you both had eyes only for each other. That bond that has been so strong between you is unbroken. Even in death, she lives in you now."

Landra searched Asha's face as she rose slowly, watching her wipe away her tears, and her heart ached as Asha leaned forward to kiss Rowan's forehead and whisper her final words.

"Rowan, Rowan, my old friend, a piece of my spirit dies with you. We part for now, but I do not doubt that one day we will stand together again."

The following day, Lord Alfred's men and the Womara women built platforms from the limbs of trees, notched and lashed together, to drag behind the horses. The bodies of the slain warriors were placed side by side, three abreast, with arms enfolded over a sword or bow. Lord Alfred, along with his men and the remaining Womara, departed the battlefield in single file. Landra glanced back at the open meadow, littered with the bodies of the raiders, as the crows descended, fighting for the spoils of the dead.

The sullen warriors rode silently through meadows filled with alpine flowers—a solemn procession moving toward the trails in the trees, and then on to the forest where their home was. The journey was slow, but when the group camped that night, the outline of the great trees in the distance gave them comfort. Landra stood with Asha, massaging her stiff neck, watching the camp settle, and posting guards around the bodies.

"You are weary, Landra. You must rest now," Asha said.

"I feel nothing but heartache," Landra answered, as she glanced at her mother's solitary form on a single platform in the center of the other women. "At least the dead will sleep closer to the forest tonight."

Asha shivered. "Their spirits will follow us until we return them home."

Clusters of men and women huddled around the fires. The chill air was heavy with the death that surrounded them. Alfred walked among the campsites, checking his men, then sought out Landra, who was keeping a vigil close to her mother.

"You must eat. Come join me at my fire and share a meal. Let us get to know each other better."

Landra glanced at Asha, who said, "I will stay close." Landra followed Alfred to his fire, seated herself across from him, and accepted the food he offered. They ate in silence for a while, before Alfred broke the stillness.

"It is unfortunate that this threat to our lands must be the circumstances of our first meeting. I am the first of our clansmen to witness the prowess of your fighting women. There is no doubt that without your march to block the barbarians and hold them back, the invasion of these northern regions would have succeeded."

Landra nodded. "We were untested in battle, but we fought for our survival. You and your people would have done no less."

"Yes, we would have fought," Alfred replied. "But you and I are young leaders, and I have not yet faced the full weight of such a sacrifice. It is a heavy toll to bear."

Landra stiffened her back as she viewed the silhouette of Asha in the firelight, next to the body of her mother.

Alfred quickly added, "We will not know what destruction has occurred along the southern coasts yet, but those clans would have had more warning and are prepared for coastal raids."

Landra pushed her plate aside. "These raiders were shrewd and probed for vulnerability, knowing the coastal defense was the strongest. It was a cunning move to climb the impenetrable cliffs of the coast and then travel overland to the north."

"Indeed," Alfred said. "Your mother's presence of mind to

send messengers to warn the clans saved many lives. It would be a dark day if they had taken the North—we would be the ones now enslaved or lying rotting in the fields. The sacrifice of your warriors will be heralded by all clans. I assure you that."

"I am grateful, my lord, but we cannot survive on praise alone," Landra replied.

Alfred recoiled at her strong words. "The death of your mother makes you bitter, I understand."

"My mother was a warrior. She is the first of our kind."

"Your kind?"

"Women who live with a mandated right to the freedoms that all men claim, and a vow to die if it is necessary to protect that freedom."

Landra watched Alfred stiffen and shift his body uncomfortably at her impassioned sentiments. She softened her words. "I have never sat with a man and talked about these things," she confessed.

"It is a different exchange for me also," Alfred said. "But your words are not lost on me. I know that you wish for a new path for your people, and you are right to press me."

"Forgive my bluntness, Lord Alfred. I do not know any other way. But how can the words of one man change the minds of many?" Landra asked.

"What is it that you seek, Landra of the Womara—to change men's minds?" Alfred asked.

Landra leaned toward him. "No, I seek the permanent rights to our lands," she said unflinchingly. She watched Alfred lean back to study her face.

"It is a bold request," he said as he eyed her. "There will be men who will challenge that claim, and contest that these lands are not mine to give. . . . However, I will take your wish under consideration."

"That is not enough." Landra sat upright. "I ask that when you return to your home, you champion our cause. Those who do not know of us will challenge such a demand from a clan of women. Time will be against us, and men will soon forget our act. They will not mourn the death of a few hundred rebel women."

Alfred nodded. "I will give you my word."

"I trust your word, but will you stay with us when we bury our dead?" Landra asked. "Then I will journey back with you to stand before your clan leaders and let them judge our worth for themselves. We cannot wait, as our deeds lose sway each day."

"Are you prepared for what they may ask in exchange?"

Landra squared her shoulders. "What more could they ask for? We have given our blood. In exchange, I will propose that we rebuild our defenses together. This invasion has been a warning call, and we must unify. You need us."

"You speak from the heart, Landra, and there is a strength to your words," Alfred replied, and paused for a moment, before adding, "We will stay with you and mourn at your fires together, and then I will stand beside you before the clan leaders."

Landra rose and placed her hand on her heart. "A new beginning from the ashes of our loved ones," she said, smiling weakly.

The next day, they moved into the interior of the ancient Womara forest and the groves of giant trees, the silent sentinels and the heart of the clan. The men stood with wide eyes, gazing around them as they viewed the homes built within the trees and in the canopies above. The Womara women and children who had hidden deep within the forest from the raiders had returned to find their homes safe, but now stood grim-faced as the procession moved slowly into a clearing and the shadows of dusk descended.

Women wept openly at the sight of Rowan upon her funeral pyre. Children sobbed when they sighted their dead mothers and were restrained from running to their sides. Lord Alfred trembled involuntarily, as if he had entered a place as solemn as any crypt. The wooden platforms holding the Womara's dead warriors were placed in a circle radiating out from the body of Rowan, who was raised above them.

"Say your farewells," Landra said, as the women moved among the dead, touching faces, speaking quietly, kissing frozen lips, and pressing flowers into rigid hands.

Landra shook as she received the funeral torch and lingered by her mother before she lit the pyre. As the flames grew, she returned to stand by Asha and Lord Alfred.

"Farewell, Mother," she whispered. "May your spirit be at peace."

7

A TRADE OF HEARTS

Day broke as a dull gray while the sound of crows calling out their warnings echoed through the trees. Landra stood before the smoldering mound of the funeral pyre, which was nothing more than the ashes of her mother and the other fallen Womara warriors. She signaled to Asha and the half-dozen women who would accompany her to mount their horses for the journey with Lord Alfred and his men.

I leave today, Mother, but I will return soon to take your ashes into the deep forest, to your final resting place. I need your spirit with me as I go to stand before the clans of men.

The Womara arrived at the lord's township a day later, under a flag of victory and to the cheers of the people, and would remain the personal guests of Lord Alfred for more than a month. Lord Alfred was true to his word and summoned the clan leaders of the surrounding regions, as well as that of the largest southern clan, to his council table to measure the destruction of the invasion.

The coastal regions had suffered the loss of property and many lives defending the coastline, but all the clansmen agreed that had the Womara not held back the raiders at the northern boundaries, all would have been lost.

In spite of that overriding truth, the opposition against allowing the women sovereignty over the region where they lived was strong. Alfred's support was the lone, impassioned argument in favor of granting lands to the Womara, while others openly voiced their dissent. Landra sat rigidly with Asha at her side, listening to the opinions of men who could decide their fate.

"What do they bring in exchange for this gift of land?" a clansman of the South argued.

"They have already given enough," Alfred said sharply.

"No more than other clans lost! And you will allow this tribe of women dominion over their lives if you grant them the status of a clan," the clansman said, raising his voice. "They are the descendants of slaves who proclaim that they have earned their right to freedom."

Landra clenched her jaw at words that cut like a knife, and Asha reached out with a cautionary touch of her arm.

Alfred rose from the table. "They earned their freedom long ago through the act of survival, thriving in a habitat no others could tame. We as clansmen of these regions no longer hold to any act of enslavement."

The men nodded their agreement and rapped the tables before them.

"So, are you guilty of judging them merely because they are women? You must set aside your prejudices, for you did not witness what I did at the battle. They fought as fiercely as any man," Alfred continued.

"It will be an ill-fated day when we grant this demand," the clansman argued. "Need I remind you that they are only one generation away from escaped slaves and outcasts? They are not clanspeople yet."

Landra rose from her seat. "I must contest your words, my lord. You judge us by preconceived notions of times now past," she challenged. "We may not accommodate your beliefs of what a clan should be, but still, we exist."

Landra walked before the men. "The invasion we have just thwarted calls upon us to consider our borders and unite to assure our future survival. We eluded death and lived to see a new day, but we cannot be self-righteous in that victory."

Lord Alfred spoke up: "I agree with Landra's words. These women warriors are the clan that will guard the northern peaks."

Landra turned back to the men. "I know that we can live with our differences, and the Womara offer something in exchange for our lands. We pledge our defense to the mountains and the coastal access across the plains of the eastern regions. We have proven our worth with the lives of our people. Our warriors will continue to scout the wild regions of these lands for the protection of all."

The men leaner closer to one another, whispering among themselves.

"In return for that security, we ask for assurance that we will have a home," Landra continued.

"And who can grant these lands?" the southern clansman asked.

The men's voices grew louder as they openly argued, before Lord Alfred raised his hand for quiet. "My region is the largest of our realms, and the Womara lands are included in those outlying boundaries. Their territory is on the fringes of the wilds and has been judged to be of little value to any commerce."

"Yes, but has that value ever been fully gauged? Once given away, it will not be able to be retrieved," one man said.

"Everything has little value until it is wanted by someone else," Landra said. "These lands have lain untouched for centuries, known only to a few nomadic tribes that move through its woods and mountains. We have grown to love the forests. I was born there, and it is a part of who we are. There is no other place for us."

The men stood silently, staring at her.

Alfred stepped forward. "All the clans from the North have a voice in this decision, but mine is still the deciding factor. I ask for an agreement for the sake of unity, but I would reward the Womara on their heroism alone. The decree will be binding and recognized by all clans. It will grant the Womara their lands and recognition of their place among us as a clan."

Landra glanced nervously at Asha.

"I will hear the 'ayes' to that decree," Alfred asked.

The "ayes" rang out; only a single "nay" was voiced, by the southern clan leader.

Landra's stomach fluttered at Lord Alfred's final words, as he spoke directly to her. "I add my final vote to those in agreement. The lands are granted to the Womara people, and from this day forward they are named a clan."

Landra eyes welled, and she blinked back tears as she looked at Asha, who beamed at her and said, "Your mother is smiling today! You have secured us our home."

Lord Alfred stepped forward to grasp her forearm. "This is a new day." He smiled. "I am glad for you."

"Thank you, my lord." She bowed her head, hand on heart.

Each clansman stepped forward and grasped her forearm in congratulations. The clansman of the South stepped forward but did not offer his hand, only hard words: "It is your challenge to prove that you are worthy of your place among us."

"I will," she answered, standing taller.

At the banquet dinner that evening, the Womara and the clansmen toasted many rounds to their new goodwill and the victory of battle. Landra sat at Lord Alfred's side and felt a little light-headed, either from the elation she still felt after the day's events or from too much wine, as he offered some advice.

"The treaty document will be drawn up in the next several days, but I hope that you will not leave in haste," he said. "You are welcome to stay among us for as long as you wish. Let my people get to know you better and foster the goodwill that you and your warriors have rightly earned."

Landra looked around the long tables at Asha and her warriors, mingling with the men, laughing and talking. *I have not fully grasped the magnitude of this treaty or our new status. It is a strange feeling to sit among these men as a clan member, but my confidence is emboldened as I consider what this could mean for my people.*

"I believe we shall stay for a time, my lord," Landra answered Alfred, with a smile.

As she and Asha walked to their quarters at the end of the evening, Asha asked. "So, we stay?"

Landra stopped and said, with a sweeping gesture of her hand, "Look around us. We need innovation to build our village into a township such as this. It is progress that we now must bring to our clan."

"What are your thoughts?" Asha asked.

"We lack skills and must trade for everything we require. What if we could acquire some of these men's trade expertise? I will start tomorrow in the marketplace to evaluate the feasibility of that prospect."

Landra paused for a moment and ordered, "And you must go with me."

Asha nodded but turned away abruptly.

"What is it?" Landra asked.

"You just remind me so much of your mother," Asha answered. "I cannot believe that she is gone. Nothing will ever be the same for me."

Landra eyes clouded with tears, as she said, "I miss her, too, and wish she had lived to witness this day."

Asha drew her close and placed her arm around her shoulders. "You have won a great victory for our people, and everything we do from this point on will honor her spirit. We must remember that."

Landra smiled. "I am glad that you are here with me. There is so much to see in this township, and I will need your counsel. We must garner all the knowledge that these people have to offer in the time we have here."

"I have faith in you," Asha said, squeezing Landra tightly. "You will find a way."

Lord Alfred informed her that the townspeople would accommodate any of the Womara's inquiries, and Landra made a point of ensuring that the Womara women became a common sight among the townspeople. They frequented the marketplace, the center and heartbeat of commerce and trade, as she asked for introductions to most of the town's merchants. They were cautious but polite, viewing her with an equal amount of curiosity.

"I have sought out most of the merchants with skills that I think will prove helpful for our instruction," she shared with Asha. "But if not for Lord Alfred's command, I am not certain that they would be so obliging."

"We cannot blame them entirely, Landra," Asha offered. "We stand out in sharp contrast with the women of this township, dressed in our men's clothing and armed with weapons."

"These are the clothes that are practical for us," Landra protested.

Asha laughed. "Certainly, but when I watch you from across the open market, you move like a man with a confident gait. Were we not under the protection of Lord Alfred, I am certain that we would encounter a challenge or two about whether we are 'real' women."

"It is not possible to blend in, nor do I want to," Landra said, glancing down at her clothing. She was dressed in leggings and a rust-colored tunic that fell to her mid-thigh. Her upper bodice was a leather vest, and her arms were partially bare. Upon her wrists, she wore leather guards for the bow and quill that hung from her back, and she carried a short sword on her hip.

"Maybe I could remove my bow," she offered, shrugging her shoulders.

Asha smiled at her. "You would still be the most distinctive of us all, with hair the color of polished bronze and hues of red that shine in the sun. I have seen nothing like it here, among these people."

"And what of you, Asha, with skin the color of dark night? *Now* who stands out?" Landra asked, laughing.

Asha nodded. "I am a strong reminder of our clan's days as slaves."

"We are free women in every sense," Landra said, "but I do think the townsfolk are starting to accept us, and we will continue to use this time of obligatory goodwill to our advantage."

Landra and Asha made their way across the open marketplace and stopped to discuss the merchants they had met at the various shops offering goods and sevices.

"I have placed women with the leather, glassworks, pottery, tailors, and animal-husbandry merchants who said they were willing to let them observe," Landra said. She turned to Asha and added, "I want you to find out how they move their goods to other markets, and where they trade."

"And you?" Asha asked, as Landra looked across the square to the forge, where a young blacksmith stood stoking the flames of his fire pit, heating the lump of metal ore, and wiping a sweaty forehead with his free hand.

"The blacksmith offers the most value," Landra mused. "Just think how much would change for us if we could make our own weapons!"

Asha nodded her agreement as Landra left to cross the square. She watched the smith look up from his work to meet her eye as she walked in his direction. But he quickly cast his gaze downward, returning to the metal on the anvil, and resumed hammering the cooling ore as she stopped before his bench. He glanced up again but did not speak as he continued to pound the metal. Landra shifted her stance, waiting patiently for the hammering to stop, before stepping closer to him, forcing him to look up and into her eyes.

"I am Landra, of the Womara," she said. She placed her hand

above her heart, bowing her head slightly but never taking her eyes from his.

"I know who you are," he replied, standing upright. "How may I help you?"

"I am interested in your trade. Might I watch you?"

"What?" he answered, setting his hammer down.

"Pardon my directness," Landra measured her words. "What is your name, may I ask?"

"Edric of Kendril," he replied.

"I know that township," Landra answered. "It lies to the south. So, you are not from here?"

Edric raised an eyebrow. "You are very curious. I am an apprentice in this town," he replied. "I am bound to this master smith for a short time more."

Landra looked down at the work on the anvil. "You are fashioning an arrow point. Can you show me how to do that?" she asked. "How long does it take to learn?"

"I am not sure how to answer that question, milady," he said, grinning. "Why do you want to know?"

"We have no skills such as yours. We seek training," Landra answered candidly. "This trade would be a great value to my people."

Edric laughed out loud but stopped abruptly.

Landra flushed, stepping toward him. "Is it because I am a woman that you laugh?" she challenged him.

"Forgive my outburst," Edric replied. "You have caught me off guard." He stepped back and eyed her in earnest. "I do not wish to offend, but I question the logic of a woman learning the black-smith's trade."

"Why, because no one has asked it of you before?" Landra

answered sharply. "It is not understandable to you that I would want to better the lives of my clanswomen?"

Edric stood before her silently, still looking at her intently. Landra felt her pulse quicken under his scrutiny but soon composed herself. "To make small items such as knives, nails, tools . . . That would greatly benefit us. In time we could learn to make more: tips for our arrows, weapons . . ."

"Has your new treaty not made your people a more secure clan? What need have you for more weapons?"

"Without the weapons that we gained in trade, we would not have been able to defend our home. Even with this new treaty, we cannot forget how easily we could have lost. We must become more resourceful," Landra said.

Edric listened to her words but gave her no answer.

"I ask that you consider my request. I will return tomorrow. I wish only to watch," she declared.

She turned to leave but felt herself flush again as she imagined his eyes watching her walk away.

Landra waited at his stall the following morning and watched Edric stop to view the Womara woman sitting at the bench of the leatherworker. He shook his head as he walked briskly toward her.

"Ah, here you wait," he said, with irritation in his voice.

"I said I would be here," Landra replied.

"I thought you might be asking in jest, but I see that you spoke in earnest. I have learned that you have made similar inquiries around the marketplace, targeting certain trades and asking to place a Womara woman with any cooperative merchant."

"Yes, I was forthright in my request to you, and you have seen the cooperation with the other merchants," Landra said. "What is your answer?"

Edric glanced around the market square. "Well, I am placed at your disposal, am I not? It would be hard not to extend the same courtesy to you that the others have," he answered.

Landra felt her face brighten at his words.

"I see no harm in your watching, but stay out of my way," he added.

Landra came every day to watch Edric work. Each morning as she crossed the market square, she heard the strike of the hammer on the small anvil, ringing like a bell through the morning stillness.

I cannot confess to Asha that I am starting to look forward to more than just his daily instructions.

She stopped a short distance away to observe him. His brow furrowed as he concentrated on the strike of metal over a horn to bend a tool, creating a spattering of hot sparks.

He has been patient and answered my questions as best he can, despite my limited expertise.

Occasionally, he allowed her to hold the hammer and tongs to shape a piece of the metal herself. She could barely hold his hammer to make the strike. When Edric stepped behind her body to help better position her arm, she caught herself holding her breath. She quickly struck the metal hard to shake the feeling. When she missed, she grimaced.

"Do not judge yourself too harshly," Edric said. "I will not admit how many times my own strike has been off."

Landra smiled weakly. "I can appreciate the years it took

you to reach such a skill level," she confessed. "I have watched you fashion a knife for days and know that even a simple tool is beyond me."

When Edric looked up from the task and smiled at her, she felt her heart skip a beat. "Well, that is enough humiliation for one day," she said, attempting to jest, and making a hasty departure.

The next day, Landra brought Asha to watch Edric and shared her candid thoughts. "It is not possible to acquire this skill with so little time," she concluded. "It is more challenging than I envisioned. I was overzealous about our people's ability to learn quickly. This was folly on my part."

"It was a good folly," Asha said. "Is it not enough that you have imagined cultivating these skills for our people? Some of the women have gained useful knowledge here, and that is a start. Give it time, and we will find a way."

"We would need to leave some women here to train," Landra said.

"Who would want to stay among this township of men for long?" Asha asked. "It would be better to bring them to us."

Landra stepped back in surprise. "Bring them to us? How so?"

"I remember many years ago when the women of the clan stood before your mother, seeking balance through the inclusion of men in their lives. It seems that we cannot completely live without them," Asha said, smiling coyly. "Your mother knew it was a time for change, and that was when we allowed the outsiders to our fires. Why not invite them again, but for a different purpose and for longer? Can you not consider a compromise again for the benefit of the clan?"

"Is that possible that men might consider living among us?" Landra asked. "And what could we offer for such an exchange?"

As the ring of the hammer sounded, Landra turned toward its source. Her eyes lingered upon Edric, his forearm muscles taut with the effort of bending the metal.

"Maybe there are more things to consider besides the exchange of money," Asha suggested. "I overheard the blacksmith speak of you with favorable words to another merchant."

"What did he say?" Landra asked.

"He spoke of your spirit and explained that you were a warrior, and that Lord Alfred's men who returned from the battle described you as a fierce fighter. He questioned his own courage to face down the charging hordes. I think he admires you."

Landra stiffened. "What do I care what he thinks?"

"You *do* care," Asha answered. "I think you like him."

Landra stared at her. "What do you mean?"

"You like him *that* way." Asha smiled.

"I do not know what you are saying. I—I—I admire him," Landra stammered. "He is a man of merit, worthy of my respect."

"Worthy of your bed," Asha answered, laughing at Landra's flushed face. "How many times have you danced at the fires, Landra?"

"Enough to know that I do not understand why mating with a man is spoken of in such glowing words. I think the experience is not worth talking about."

"That is because you were only curious with those men," Asha said, glancing at Edric. "He will be different for you. You are attracted to him even if you cannot yet recognize your own desires."

Landra frowned, watching Edric as he plunged a piece of metal into the water bucket and the steam rose around him.

"He is a strong man, and worthy of you. Go to his bed," Asha urged. She reached out and lifted Landra's chin. "Put your grief aside for a while and escape the burden of worrying about all of us."

Landra turned to watch Edric a moment longer, then slowly shook her head. "I cannot," she said, before walking away.

That afternoon, Landra sought out Lord Alfred to announce that she and the clanswomen would depart the following day. She shared her sincere gratitude for his support and her heartfelt allegiance to their common goal of continued goodwill.

Departing Lord Alfred's hall, she told Asha, "I must take my leave of Edric. I owe him my thanks."

As she walked across the marketplace, toward the blacksmith's stall, she felt her stomach grip when she heard the familiar ring of the hammer. Edric stopped his work as she approached, removing his apron and stepping out to greet her. "I hear a rumor that you and your women will depart tomorrow," he said.

Landra stood silently, shifting uncomfortably. "Yes, and I came because I wanted to express my gratitude to you for the time you have given me."

Edric smiled, leaning closer. "You have surprised me, Landra. You have been a most attentive student, and I have been impressed with your questions. Your curiosity and willingness to learn will serve your people well."

Landra felt herself flush at his praise.

"I am glad that you have come to say your goodbye. I have something for you," he said. He walked back to his bench, retrieved a bundle wrapped in cloth, and handed it to her.

Landra unwrapped it to find the knife that she had watched

him craft the week before. She felt her eyes go wide. "Thank you," she said, as she turned it over in her hands, admiring the artistry. "It is a beautiful gift."

"It is a gift worthy of the warrior that you are," Edric said.

Landra's heart began to beat more rapidly as she felt his eyes upon her. *I wish there was something I could leave him as a remembrance of me.* "It is I who should give you something in return for your patience," she managed.

Edric did not take his eyes from hers as he spoke. "Our time together is gift enough. It has been my privilege to know you."

Landra looked down at his workbench and reached out to touch one of the tools while she composed herself. "And what of you? I have not asked of your final plans, Edric."

"What do you wish to know?"

"Will you return to your township?"

"I am undecided," Edric replied. "I like the North, but there are more than enough smiths here. The townships to the south may have a greater need for my skills."

Landra nodded, shifting her stance again, glancing over her shoulder at Asha, who stood waiting for her.

"Then I will take my leave and bid you farewell, Edric. I wish you well."

"And to you as well, Landra."

Landra turned to walk away but stopped and turned slowly back to him. "I wish to propose a different venture," she said.

"What do you mean?" Edric asked.

"We need your knowledge," Landra said. "We cannot learn your trade in few months or even years. I would like to offer you a place among us where your skills will be valued. You will be the first to bring trade to our clan."

Edric's eyes flashed. "Live among you?"

"Yes," Landra said, stepping closer to him. "Or somewhere nearby of your choice. We cannot pay you, but we can give you lodging and food in exchange for your teachings. We will build you a home and provide for your needs. Here, you are one among many, but among us you will provide value to many more, as well as a new beginning for my people."

Edric looked at her thoughtfully. "Are you certain that you wish me to be that man?"

"You would be the first," Landra said, smiling hopefully. "I know I have shocked you with my directness, and I understand that you may want time to consider my words."

"In truth, I do not know what to say," Edric answered. "But I do have some questions of you."

"Yes, of course."

"Every day you have come to ask your questions, watching and learning from me. Will all your women be as eager learners as you are?"

"Yes, they will," she said.

Edric pondered her statement for a moment, then said, "I do not think that will be enough."

Landra lowered her head, feeling her chest tighten at his words, until he stepped closer to her and explained himself: "For what you do not know is that I have come to look forward to your presence every single day. It will be difficult not to have you near."

"But I *will* be near," Landra answered, wondering if he could hear her pounding heart.

Edric smiled and touched her arm. "You misunderstand my meaning. I have learned of the Womara ways and your fire rites."

"Yes." She searched his face. "You would be welcome to attend the fires as part of the clan, if you desired."

"I want more, Landra. I want a mate, and it is you I desire, no other. Your offer is compelling because I would be with you in your world."

Landra felt her pulse quicken as Edric took her hands in his. "It is an exchange of hearts that I ask of you. So now it is you who must consider my request."

The noise of the market square around them faded away, until she could see nothing besides the deep recesses of his eyes shining before her.

"It is a difficult time to talk about the heart, for mine still bleeds for the loss of my mother."

Edric's eyes flinched.

"But it is also a time for healing," she added, smiling at him as she grasped his hands more tightly.

"Come to my forest, and let us see where our hearts take us."

8

THE PORT OF LORD EDMOND

Over the next few hours, the crew readied the ship's cargo as the coastline and port of Lord Edmond drew closer. Seanna was in her quarters belowdecks, packing the few possessions she had carried with her and listening to the men on the deck rushing back and forth as the captain shouted orders from his station.

She opened a soft purple cloth to look at the moonstone necklace inside, a gift from James, and ran her fingers along the silver chain, letting her touch linger on the smooth stone. Her skin tingled at the thought of James's touch when he had placed it around her neck the first time.

The shouts of the crew above interrupted her thoughts, and she rewrapped the present hastily. Leaving her quarters, she descended to the bottom deck, where her horse was penned. Her mare reared her head and whinnied her greeting as Seanna patted her nose affectionately.

"I know, I know . . . I am excited to be home, too. You will be off this ship soon, and in a short time we will walk among the trees of our forest again."

The mare nuzzled her nose more deeply into Seanna's hand, making Seanna laugh. "I think that you have done enough traveling for a lifetime, my old friend. What adventures we have shared. Do you sense the quiet forest meadows that await you?" Seanna rubbed the mare's brow wistfully. "No tranquil meadows for me, as I must take my place at the table of men as a messenger to the alliance."

She kissed her mare's soft muzzle. "But no more talk of duty. We are almost home!"

The boat anchored off Lord Edmond's port, and the rowboats ferried the passengers toward the docks. Seanna stood at the front of the lead boat, from which she could make out the outline of people gathering at the dock to welcome them. Lord Orman and his entourage followed in a second boat as they rowed toward the landing, and the contours of faces ashore grew more distinct.

Seanna saw her longtime ally and friend Lord Stuart, the son of Lord Edmond, waiting for her on the docks. The boat crew pulled hard on the oars, moving her close enough for Stuart to catch her eye and raise his hand in greeting.

What a joy to see my old friend again, she thought as she waved back.

Seanna's eyes widened as she then saw her friend Thea move forward to stand at Stuart's side, both hands clasped over her heart in her and Seanna's special greeting. Seanna beamed, returning the gesture.

As the boats drew alongside the dock, Stuart extended a hand

and grasped her forearm tightly, steadying her as she disembarked. "Seanna, my friend, it is good to see you again."

"And you, my lord," Seanna replied, embracing him warmly before turning to Thea and doing the same. "I have missed you both," she said. "Thea, I am surprised that you are here. It is wonderful to see you, but was this welcome planned for me?" she asked.

Thea grinned. "Only in part. When I left you on the mountain, I traveled here at the invitation of Lord Stuart and have remained while you were gone."

Seanna lifted an eyebrow at Thea's words, and Thea shrugged her shoulders—a silent message that they would talk later, in private. Seanna remembered herself as she glanced over Thea's shoulder at Lord Orman's boat. The envoy was assisted onto the dock and began making his way toward her. Her stance stiffened slightly as Orman stopped before them.

"Lord Orman, may I introduce you to Lord Stuart, son of Lord Edmond, clan leader of this region," Seanna said.

"It is my honor, sir," Orman said, bowing low.

"Lord Orman is the special envoy appointed by King James and the king's council to represent their kingdom and begin discussions of a proposed trade route," Seanna explained.

"It is our honor to welcome you to our region, Lord Orman," Stuart said. "And may I introduce Thealia, of the Womara clan."

Thea stepped forward, placing her hand upon her heart and bowing her head. "Welcome, Lord Orman," she said, as Orman bowed politely in return.

"I hope your journey was pleasant," Stuart continued.

"It was acceptable," Lord Orman answered.

"That is a very well-mannered answer," Seanna interrupted, laughing. "Lord Orman must have fared better than I. My affinity for water does not extend to the open sea, and having my feet upon firm land again is a relief."

Stuart smiled. "Well, then let us not linger. My father awaits our arrival in the meeting hall. Please follow me," he directed, with a sweep of his hand.

Thea took Seanna's arm, squeezing it and giving her a mischievous sideways glance while speaking under her breath: "Well, you certainly have stirred things up. What an entrance!"

Orman walked briskly alongside Stuart, followed by the men in his entourage. Stuart was giving sweeping descriptions of the current port and township as Orman nodded, half listening. He was more interested in the people that lived here. When they had rowed in to the dock, he had watched from his perspective behind Seanna's boat while she had disembarked into the waiting embrace of her friends.

Now that I am here, I can observe her people firsthand. Do you change when you are among your kind, Seanna?

The young man who greeted her on the dock was Lord Stuart, the son and heir of Lord Edmond. Orman had not recognized the imposing woman at his side, but her attire—a long-sleeved green tunic with darker leggings underneath and high leather boots, and a weapon on her hip—had led him to surmise that she was a Womara.

The dark-haired one is too young to be the clan leader. Is she Lord Stuart's woman? It appears that Seanna's mother has not journeyed here to welcome us.

When he was introduced to Thea, he noted her beauty. Her

thick auburn hair fell below her waist; a silver clasp held a single thin braid at her temple. Her eyes were amber, and she had the same direct gaze as Seanna. She stood tall at Stuart's side, not demurely behind. Orman kept his expression as open and welcoming as possible, as he realized, *I know I am being examined, and I welcome the opportunity to observe these women in return. Can they all be as self-controlled as Seanna is?*

The township fanned out from the small port, and the market center was within walking distance of the docks. Orman compared this area's smaller scope with his kingdom's port and thought of the imposing amount of commerce that flowed through his region's docking areas. The expansion to accommodate more trade would be an immediate boon to Edmond's township.

At the far end of the breakwater was a sheltered cove where Orman could see what looked like a stone rampart being constructed. Many men, naked from the waist up, stood chest high in the water, picking up rocks large enough to carry and placing them at the water's edge.

"I see you have begun some expansion, Lord Stuart," Orman said. He turned to Seanna. "You did not tell me that they had begun building."

"I was not aware that they had," Seanna answered.

"We work to reinforce the foundation," Stuart replied.

Eager to begin progress. I cannot fault them that, Orman thought.

"I believe that the men who have accompanied me on this journey might offer suggestions in the construction of your port."

"That would be greatly appreciated, Lord Orman," Stuart answered.

"Well, of course, if you are under the directive of your alliance to begin construction. I am the envoy for my king to your alliance and an observer, but your port appears to have great possibilities. And are there no other ports along your coastline to expand?"

Orman watched Seanna's eyes narrow at his comment before Stuart deflected his question: "The alliance has deemed our port the best location for a new trade route."

Orman smiled to himself. *It is good to raise expectations about discussions of the port and then temper them. The leaders will be more apt to concession, as I hold the advantage for those who wish to gain my favor.*

At the town's center stood a long hall, and inside was a gathering of Lord Edmond's subjects and a representation of the clan leaders from the outlying areas waited. Lord Edmond rose slowly from his seat as Orman, Seanna, Stuart, and Thea entered, not allowing his manservant to assist him in standing beside his chair. He straightened his stance and squared his shoulders with the pride befitting a once-powerful clan leader.

Orman judged him to be a tall man for his age, in spite of the slight rounding of his posture, but the lord could not disguise his frailty as he reached for the arm of his son, who had joined him at his side, to steady him. His brown hair and beard were laced with gray. His skin looked taut, drawn over prominent cheekbones, and his dark eyes, slightly sunken in their sockets, made him appear skeletal. He was a man at the end of his prime.

Orman had learned from the spies he had sent to the region that Lord Edmond was a fair leader, possessed of an even temperament and blessed with the affection of his people. But the surrounding clansmen already looked to the son as the future of their people.

Stuart stepped forward. "Father, I wish to introduce Lord Orman, envoy to King James of the city of Bathemor."

"It is an honor to meet you, Lord Orman," Edmond said.

"Thank you, my lord, but the honor is mine," Orman answered.

Edmond smiled as he turned his attention to Seanna, who stood at Orman's side. She stepped forward and dropped to one knee before him, her hand over her heart. "My lord."

Lord Edmond smiled. "All these formalities. Stand up and come closer. Let me see you," he said, placing his hands upon her shoulders affectionately. "Welcome home, Seanna."

"Thank you, my lord."

After more introductions among the more prominent clan leaders and citizens, glasses of wine were poured and Lord Stuart toasted to the safe arrival of his honored guests from a new region. Seanna and Thea stood beside him and lifted their glasses as Orman watched them.

The Womara woman Thealia is rumored to be Stuart's future wife, and one not of his clan. I am curious whether that union has garnered any dissent. That marriage would certainly solidify the alliance between this southern clan and the Womara to the north. What do the other clans think of such a solidarity? And what of James and Seanna? Would that be an even more powerful union?

After the meal was served, the leaders of the surrounding clans and the men of Edmond's court were eager to begin the discussions with the mappers and the proposed coastal route, but Orman skillfully deferred any discussions. He was measured in his words, determined not to reveal too much information, and only alluded to the discussions that he had had with his own council. He would not speak to any facts or acknowledge that Lord Edmond's township was the best choice for any linked trade ports, and said he would defer outcomes until the pending meeting with the alliance council.

The king has indicated that he favors Lord Edmond's township because they are allies of the Womara. But I will meet with the alliance council and judge their temperaments regarding other alternatives, if they should exist, as I have heard they might.

He had to admit that he enjoyed seeing the men's hopes deflated at his hints of postponements in any talk until he traveled north. "Gentlemen, I must do my duty as envoy to our region and meet with your alliance. I understand that there are others who will want to offer their input," he said, as he watched the men exchange disappointed looks.

"Let us not diminish this auspicious occasion with speculation," he added. "Allow me to be the first to raise my glass to the fact that we stand here today, on the cusp of this historic beginning."

Orman watched Stuart, across the room, lean in to speak in his father's ear. Lord Edmond nodded and signaled for Seanna to draw near, and she talked in earnest as the older lord listened.

Lord Edmond values her confidence. I am sure the old bull is not subject to flattery or idle words, nor would Seanna offer such wasted frivolity. What does she counsel him on?

When Orman was summoned over to speak with the lord, they agreed that he, Lord Stuart, and some of the regional clans' leaders would journey the next day to the township of Lord Arden, to meet with the alliance council.

Orman forced a smile when Seanna informed him that she and the Womara women would also depart the following day, but for their home. Seanna took her leave of him with feigned pleasantry and hollow words about looking forward to their reunion when they rendezvoused later at Lord Arden's court.

She makes haste to return to her own lands. I am disappointed not to be able to travel to the Womara valley and the peaks beyond, and to view the location of the pass. Maybe at a later time—although, if that is up to Seanna, I think not.

As the evening waned, Seanna stood close to her fellow Womara, engaged in animated conversations, and Orman watched them with great curiosity, wondering, *What is it that makes them stand apart?*

Seanna and her friend Thea were beauties, and the other Womara plainer in their appearance, but that was not what distinguished them. As a group, they exuded an almost animal magnetism; even the fact that they were women did not diminish their power. They reminded him of a pack of wolves—splendid animals alone, but deadly in the hunt.

9

HOMEWARD

At dawn, Seanna and two other scouts checked their packed horses before mounting to depart Lord Edmond's township, their destination the Womara valley. Seanna turned in surprise when she saw Thea approaching, dressed for travel and leading her horse.

"I will come with you," Thea announced.

Seanna raised an eyebrow. "You are most welcome, but will Stuart not see you off?"

"We said our goodbyes earlier," Thea replied, her forehead furrowed as she looked away from Seanna's questioning expression.

Seanna did not press her for more information. "Let us go, then," she said.

The women left the inner courtyard as the servants were beginning to stir with the duties of the day. The clip-clop of the horses' hooves echoed among the stone streets as they moved through the town and out the fortress gates.

The women traveled the well-worn roads leading away from

the township until they diverted into the surrounding countryside. They passed the last scatterings of small villages and homesteads, then moved deeper into the outer territory on the less frequented trails through the woodlands and meadows.

Seanna leaned back in her saddle to look upward into the trees and at the light filtering through the dense leaves, breathing the air deeply as they fell into the rhythm of the journey. They rode all day, stopping only briefly to water the horses in the river streams. The terrain grew ever wilder as the horses moved single file along the steeper woodland trails.

Seanna's was the rear horse. As she watched the women scouts in the line riding ahead of her, she noted how the soft browns and greens of their clothing blended with the surrounding colors of the leaves and trees. Their hair was more distinct, with varying colors that reflected their diverse mixed ancestry. All of the women, including Seanna, were heavily armed, with bows and arrows, short or long swords, and knives in their back belts. The women remained vigilant as they passed through the remote woodlands.

Lulled by the gait of her horse, Seanna settled lower into her saddle, feeling reconnected with an old piece of herself. *My life has changed so quickly since I discovered the mountain pass and fell in love with James. Out here in the wilds, I know myself again, and my divided heart returns home.*

She looked down at the fallen leaves upon the trail, still wet from a rain the night before. She smelled the familiar odors of the earth, the decay in the undergrowth beneath the trees, and the musk of the moss that covered the rocks. She wrinkled her nose when she detected a faint trace of the scent from a skunk that had crossed the trail. The sounds of many birds rang from the trees, chirping in discordant song or echoed calls of warning as the scouts passed by. Her heart stirred.

I have marveled at James's city of stone, which has tamed the wilds that once surrounded it, but I still struggle to understand why men feel a need to conquer and destroy the nature around them.

Thea turned back to smile at her, and Seanna grinned back. *Part of the strength of my people is our willingness to adapt to the nature that we live in. We have survived through our ability to blend with those elements and we do not seek to dominate, and that makes me proud.*

The women made camp for the evening deep within the forest. Around the warmth of the fire, Seanna shared parts of her journey and stories about the individuals she had encountered. Her friends were curious and their questions poignant, but mostly they asked about the character of the people Seanna had met in the new region.

"What is their nature? How are they different?" the women asked.

Seanna was forthright and shared most of her experiences, except for any news of James.

"And did the women accept you?" Thea asked.

"I am not certain. I did not develop any real friendships. I think it would have taken more time, because I was such an object of curiosity."

In truth, I could not help but notice the sharp contrast between my women and those who live in James's lands. The disparities are great, and I fear that I will always be an outcast in James's world—so much so that perhaps the gulf will prove too great for us to bridge our differences.

Seanna shared the story of her confrontation with Malcolm, the king's guard who had tested her fighting skills in the arena. The woman nodded in unison when she spoke of his defeat in front of the king and many of the townspeople.

"A just outcome," Thea said.

"How did such a challenge happen?" a scout asked.

"Someone wanted to see if a woman could really fight. I suspect that Lord Orman, the envoy who has accompanied me on this voyage, goaded Malcolm, into challenging me. Malcolm may have been only Orman's puppet, but I singled him out anyway, along with four of his guards."

"You defeated them all?" the scout asked.

"Yes," Seanna answered. "But I kept Malcolm for the last, and his downfall was a personal humiliation before his people."

"Were you scorned for so thoroughly disgracing the king's guard?" Thea asked.

"No," Seanna answered, "but it was a gamble. I gained the king's favor, along with a measured degree of acceptance from the king's council. I became a champion that day because of the king's support."

The women nodded in agreement, before wrapping their cloaks around themselves and lying down before the fire. Seanna and Thea sat together, watching the flames and listening to the soft sounds of the women's breathing as they fell into sleep. Taking one more glance at the sleeping women, Seanna rested her eyes on Thea and said, "Now, tell me what troubles you." As Thea looked up to meet her gaze, Seanna added, "Your mood has changed since you greeted me at the dock at Stuart's side. I thought you might whisper that I had arrived in time for the announcement of a wedding."

Thea nodded. "And would you have been surprised?"

"Maybe, but the news would not have been unexpected. You and I have talked before about the question of marriage."

"In truth, he has asked me to be his wife," Thea said.

"And your answer?"

"I have consented," Thea answered.

"That is wonderful, Thea!" Seanna said, reaching out to hold her friend's hand. "But why no announcement before we left? And why are you here with me?"

Thea kept her eyes on the fire. "I am not certain that I can answer your questions. I am beginning to understand that love and marriage are two very different things, and an even more difficult blend for a Womara woman."

"I think I understand," Seanna answered.

"I am happy in love, but I struggle with the question of marriage to a clan leader and what is expected of me. Will I be asked to change who I am?"

"Did Stuart not want to let you go on this journey?" Seanna asked.

"*Let* me go?" Thea stiffened. "I will go when I want."

Seanna started at the hardness of her friend's words.

"Forgive me." Thea shrugged her shoulders. "Let me try to explain the cause of my ill mood."

Seanna smiled, encouraging her to continue.

"Stuart and I argued for the first time when he challenged my leaving to accompany you."

"I am sorry that you argued and that I may be the cause. Did Stuart not know in advance that you thought of leaving?" Seanna asked.

"No, I did not discuss it with him. I told him I would be gone for a moon."

"Thea, why such harshness in your words? Stuart is your betrothed."

Thea nodded. "I know. I just needed to go."

"Why did you need to go?"

Thea shrugged again. "I cannot say entirely, except that I wanted to breathe the forest air again. I wanted to be with you and feel unconstrained, like we once were in our youth."

Seanna looked into her friend's eyes, thinking, *I understand the sentiments behind her words. Have I myself not secretly questioned my ability to balance love and my autonomy?*

Thea continued, "When Stuart relented, agreeing that I should escort you and visit my home, he also announced that he would send a personal escort for my protection."

"And this is why you argued?"

"His words incensed me," Thea answered. "'Nothing has changed except that I will soon be your wife,' I told him. Her eyes flashed in the light of the fire. "That was his reason for concern: He reminded me that I was the future wife of a clan leader and said he wanted me protected."

Seanna looked around. "Well, there is no escort here to accompany us."

"No, because I reminded him that I was once his bodyguard and protected *him*," Thea said.

Seanna had no words of comfort that could lessen her friend's frustration, so they settled into silence by the fire. Thea threw more wood onto the flames as night descended into blackness, blanketing the women and the forest. A lone owl called from the trees.

Seanna smiled. "I have some news that I think will lighten your heart."

"What is it?" Thea straightened up.

"Something has changed for me."

Thea's face brightened. "On the docks when I saw you again, I sensed that something more than just a diplomatic triumph had happened. You hid your feelings in the company of men, but I know you too well. You emanated a glow, as you do now."

"Are you sure about that?" Seanna laughed. "I think it was a tinge of green in my complexion, to match my unsettled stomach from the sea journey."

Thea stopped her. "You jest, but indeed something has changed. Even now, your eyes shine in the firelight."

Seanna leaned closer. "I have found love."

Thea's eyes went wide as she reached out to take Seanna's hand. "The king proved to be the man of your heart?"

Seanna smiled. "I denied my feelings through my journey until I saw him again upon the mountain."

Thea beamed. "I am so happy for you, my friend. How could you hold this joy from me?" she admonished. "You must tell me everything now that we are alone."

"I don't even know where to begin," Seanna answered.

"Tell me of your love."

Over the next several hours, Seanna shared with Thea everything, starting from the time when James had asked her to return to his city and stand with him when they buried his father. She spoke of the deep respect between them that had grown into more. Her sentiments had turned with James's support of her after the challenge in the arena, and with his gift of the moonstone necklace, but she had struggled when she realized that she was falling in love.

"If James had not been bold enough to ask me, on our last day together, to visit his boyhood cottage, everything might be different. I was determined to leave after his father's funeral because I was confused and feared I was in danger of revealing my heart," Seanna confessed.

"But you did surrender to your heart?" Thea asked.

"There are times when I think I cannot contain my emotions and I am humbled in that joy. Then, at other times, I feel as if I have lost myself, because I never imagined I could feel such a depth of need—that I would want him so much."

Thea flashed her mischievous smile. "Tell me more."

Seanna laughed. "Your friendship allows you a certain amount of impropriety, but some things remain private."

Thea nodded knowingly.

"What did you feel when Stuart declared his love?" Seanna asked.

Thea drew her knees to her chest. "We were friends first, like you and your king, but our feelings grew over time. His words of love only confirmed what I had known in my heart all along. I know my sentiments seem strange in light of what I have just confessed."

"Not so strange. I think I understand," Seanna answered.

"Are you disappointed that you did not have the sacred fire to bless your union with James?" Thea asked.

"Did I say that I did not dance at a fire?"

Thea laughed. "Must I drag everything out of you?"

"He built a fire for us to honor our rites and waited in a meadow for me. It was a full moon and one of the most beautiful nights I have ever seen."

"I think I will like this king," Thea said.

Seanna nodded. "He is the best of men."

"And the other men who accompany you?" Thea asked. "What of his envoy? You cast a cautionary look when he approached."

"You are correct. He is not to be trusted," Seanna warned.

Thea nodded. "Your mother will measure him when they meet."

"Yes, but they should meet in the presence of Lord Arden and the alliance council. We must keep all his actions in the open. He assumes the role of a diplomat, but I am certain that he is no friend to the Womara."

Seanna and the Womara band pushed hard for the next two days. The sun was dipping low on the horizon when they emerged over hills and began their descent into the Womara valley and the final miles of their journey. A vast meadow lay before them, and the forests that bordered their homeland contrasted with the majestic peaks in the distance.

Thea called out to the group, "We shall reach the township by dark and ahead of those storm clouds."

Seanna watched the women exchange smiles and grinned back, knowing that soon they would be within their lands. They emerged from the trail at the edge of the large meadow, and the lead scout froze. In the center of the open field, kneeling in the tall grass, was a group of five men, dressing out a deer they had killed. The women placed their hands on their sword hilts as Seanna gauged who the strangers were.

The animal robes they wore implied that they were men of the nomadic tribes that roamed the upper coastal regions and foraged in small bands of twenty to thirty people. The tribe spurned contact with outsiders, making encounters unpredictable and dangerous for any man or woman who might happen upon them. Seanna searched the meadow fringes for more people as the men rose in unison, eyeing the women malevolently. They wiped their bloody hands on their pant leggings, before grasping their knives defensively.

The lead Womara scout moved forward, and the women followed in single file. When they reached the men, Seanna, Thea, and the other scouts dismounted cautiously and stood near their horses.

One of the men stepped forward. "We are not poaching here." He was taller than the rest of his kind, wearing an animal skin as a cloak. His skin and deep-set eyes were dark; his brown hair was long and matted. Even from where Seanna stood, she could smell the odor of his body. He kept his hand placed on the knife hilt that hung from his belt.

"We are not challenging your kill," Seanna answered. "But you are far from home, are you not?"

"What matter is it of yours where we travel?" he snapped.

"It is our concern if you trespass too close to our boundaries, so I will give you a warning: Take your kill, but go no farther into this valley."

Seanna watched as the men looked expectantly at their leader. He stepped closer to her and boasted, "We are five to your four."

Seanna glanced back at her women, standing ready. "That may be, but you all will die if you make a move against us," she answered.

The man spat on the ground. "You think that your kind rules this valley?"

The women scouts stiffened as they readied their swords.

"Maybe you will not all die," the leader taunted. "It would be unfortunate if one of you survived without the protection of your other women."

"Don't be a fool," Seanna said. "Do you know our decree? Violate a Womara, and you lose your life." With that, she drew her sword. "Now, for the last time, we will let you pass unharmed, but make one more threat, and it will be your last."

The men glared at the weapon in her hand as she stood unflinching, until the leader signaled to his group to back down and sputtered his final, defiant words: "There may be a day when you travel alone, and then we shall see how you fight."

Thea stepped forward. "The fight will be the same."

The men dropped to their knees, hastily finished dressing the deer, and packed their spoils. The women mounted their horses and moved slowly away, keeping the intruders in their sights until they crossed over to the other side of the meadow.

Thea spurred her horse beside Seanna. "What stupid brutes to threaten us!" she said. "I am glad that Willa was not here today. It has been many long years since nomads from a tribe like them took her."

Seanna felt a chill along her spine at the horror of that memory. "I remember the day she returned. I was just a young child, but her story became a warning call to all our women."

10

THE ABDUCTION OF WILLA

Willa limped into the Womara village, struggling to walk past a line of woman warriors who thumped their swords in unison on the ground, welcoming her back. She had endured the warrior's rite of passage for a full moon cycle deep within the wild interiors of the Womara forests, with only a single knife for protection. She grimaced as she walked into her mother's outstretched arms.

"You have returned, my daughter!" Her mother beamed as Willa smiled weakly. Her mother touched the long gash along Willa's thigh; it was still raw from her clash with a wild boar that she had stalked and killed. She had closed the wound with a needle made from a sharpened bone, biting down hard on a stick placed between her teeth as the pig's haunches cooked over a fire. She had kept herself alive by using her survival skills, cultivated since she was old enough to walk. The pain of her wound was nothing to her as she stood tall, flushed with pride at having earned her place among her fellow women, and the right to call herself a clan warrior.

Within two days of her return from the rite of passage, Willa told her mother that she intended to travel to the nearest village, a day's ride away, to trade for a new sword that she believed would be worthy of her new stature. She departed that early morning, in high spirits and traveling alone, but she would never reach her destination.

Willa stopped at a small stream to water her horse, and the snap of a twig was the only warning she heard as three men hiding among the trees set upon her. She had no chance to get her hand on her sword before they knocked her to the ground and disarmed her.

A man held her on either side, pinning her arms down. Her legs were free for a moment, and she kicked hard before the third man subdued her by laying his full body weight upon her. She arched her back in a vain attempt to pitch him off and he slapped her hard across her face before he tore down her breeches and pressed her legs apart, then penetrated her roughly.

When the man finished, he rolled off and the others released her arms. Willa crawled on her hands and knees toward her discarded weapon as they laughed.

"You have to admire her strength," the violator spoke. "She fights like a wildcat."

"I will kill you," Willa spat, as she wiped the blood from her mouth and staggered to her feet as the man moved toward her.

"Leave her. You have had your fill," one of the man said. "We must go."

"No," her rapist said. "I have no woman. I think once I have broken her, she will serve me well. I will take her with us."

Willa stumbled backward at the horror of his words, but he bound her and threw her onto the back of her horse. The men moved quickly away from the village road and into the forest trails. Willa knew from her mother's warnings that they were from the nomadic tribes that moved in small bands through the regions, shunning the life of conventional villages and townships, yet she had never encountered them before. They moved with the changing seasons, following the migration of animals. They trekked across hundreds of miles of territory but favored the rugged and isolated cliff areas of the northern coastline. The rock alcoves there were rich with seabirds, nests filled with eggs, and abundant seafood.

Willa vomited on the back of the horse, struggling to control her panic as they traveled farther away from the lands she knew. She strained to make mental maps of the terrain that they passed through over the next several days, speculating that they were making their way toward the coastal cliffs.

When they arrived at the men's makeshift camp, Willa's captors beat her before a group of thirty men, women, and children and issued a warning to the tribe to keep a close eye on her. Her violator made sure that she was never left alone and kept her hobbled day and night with ropes around her ankles. At dusk, she was tied to the pole of her captor's tent, the man who had claimed her as his woman assaulted her again and again. She fought him every time he took her.

Willa lived among them as a captive animal for almost a year, but she never gave up hope of escape. One morning, months into her captivity, she woke up, rolled over, and retched onto the ground.

"You must be with child," the man boasted.

Willa fought back tears as she felt her hardening stomach. She could not remember her last bleed. The thought of giving birth to a child magnified her desperation to get away. As she glanced wildly around the camp that was her prison, she thought, *I will never escape with a baby coming!*

She took deep breaths to calm herself and rethought her predicament. *I must use my condition to my advantage. This bastard who enslaves me has always believed he will break me with time. I must convince him and his people that I am pacified and content among them, and that the prospect of this child has led me to accept my captivity.*

Willa began making small overtures, such as rubbing her stomach contentedly and trying to smile more in her captor's company. She sought the tribal healer's advice on herbs that would help lessen her morning sickness and make her strong. She fashioned a small carrier from the skins of animals and lined it with soft fur.

Her ruses proved effective, as she was left unbound more frequently and allowed to accompany the women of the tribe as they foraged in the surrounding forests. In the lush areas where they scavenged, she learned of the flora and fauna that sustained them.

"This one is good to eat," the healer instructed, stooping low to pick a plant, handing it to Willa to examine its leaves.

"This one cleanses a wound, but beware this one. It will make you sick," the old woman said, as Willa looked at it closely.

The healer showed her the limbs of trees that bore low-hanging fruit and the hollows where the bees made their hives. Willa wove rabbit snares from supple willow branches and learned to smoke pieces of larger game, giving the nomads a steady supply of dried meat as they traveled to new regions.

The tribe moved with the seasons, and their wanderings

sharpened Willa's acuity amid her surroundings. In the colder months, they roamed the hills, woods, and open grasslands where the game was easier to hunt. She noted the landmarks of the areas they passed through, how the trees and grasses changed, and the places where the animals were most abundant.

She was hundreds of miles from her home but remained vigilant for an opening to escape as soon as the baby was born. Her hatred for her captor kept her alive, even as he mocked her, boasting to the other men that he had tamed the wild woman who bore his child. Though he disgusted her, she could not stand herself even more at times, in her feigned state of contentment. She gritted her teeth and her skin still recoiled at his rough touch and pig-like grunts whenever he took her. As she began to prepare herself for the reality of the impending birth, she realized, *If I escape, I will not hesitate to abandon this baby.*

Willa sat silently in their tent at night, listening patiently to the man's rantings, thinking she would lose her mind at times.

"All of your kind have grown soft," he chided. "You carve out the surrounding wilds, cut down the forest, clear your fields, domesticate your animals, and build your towns."

Willa never responded as he rattled on, "Your people have forgotten how to live. We are the ones who are truly free."

Does he rage because he recognizes that his people struggle against a shrinking way of life as the boundaries of civilized man close around them?

Willa's ruse as a contented expectant mother continued to be effective, and her captor grew more relaxed in the last month of her pregnancy, cutting the rope that hobbled her by day, thinking she could not run far in her condition. One morning she stepped from the tent, holding her heavy stomach in the chill air. *I shall bear this child soon.*

Her nostrils widened as she smelled the coming of winter. Soon the tribe would move on to more sheltered grounds farther away. She had overheard the man tell the others that they would leave soon, heading out of the forests to lands along the coast.

The next day, her captor announced that he would check the traps for small game before their journey and demanded that she accompany him. They walked the animals' trails, leading the horse that would carry any capture they found. In one of the rope snares was a small wild pig, its hind leg caught. It squealed in fear before the man killed it with one quick stroke. He signaled for Willa to dress out the kill as he dragged it to a clear patch in the meadow. He drew his knife and handed it to her. "Clean it, woman."

She cut the sinew around the pig's feet and slit along the legs to pull the skin free. The man turned his back to her and gazed up into the sky, his hand shielding the sun from his eyes. From her crouched position and in one quick movement, she lunged low at him, cutting his Achilles tendon. He screamed and dropped to his knees before she slashed the other tendon.

Sprawled on the ground, the man cursed her as he tried to drag himself away, then rolled to his back to watch her with wide eyes. She kept a safe distance and stood rigid before him.

"Did you think that I would never avenge my rape?" she shouted.

"You bear my child, you crazed bitch," he snarled.

"The child is innocent, but you are a savage," Willa snapped back.

"You will not get far. What do you think will happen to you when my people find me like this?"

"There will be no rescue. Only death," she said, as she lunged forward and drove the knife into his gut, dragging it upward until the blade pierced his heart, killing him instantly.

The exertion made her stomach contract, and she grabbed it protectively, standing slowly. She grabbed the reins of the horse, leading it to the dead man's body and roping his feet, then dragging the corpse to a ravine, where she rolled him down into the thickets below. She guided the horse to a large rock and steadied herself before struggling to drag herself onto its back, groaning at the effort.

Willa glanced back at the carcass of the pig. Its blood soaked the ground, along with that of the man she had dragged through the grass. A good tracker would find him in the hidden thicket, but her concealment efforts might buy her some precious time. She followed the river for as long as she could, walking the stream bed and hoping to disguise her tracks.

The next day, her water broke, soaking the back of her horse and doubling her over as the first pain of labor sent a shock wave through her body. She pressed on for as long as possible, searching the forest until she found a large tree with a hollowed-out trunk, and then lowered herself carefully from the horse, crawling within the shelter and collapsing on the dried leaves inside.

The pain was unbearable, and she bit her lip to keep herself from screaming as each new contraction gripped her body. She lay on her back and panted, unable to resist the urge to push. When she could no longer hold back, she crouched low and bore down until she felt the baby pass through the birth canal. It lay at her feet in the leaves while she cut the umbilical cord and then held the tiny body in her hands. It was a boy.

She had told herself that she would abandon the infant as soon as it was it born, but when she looked down at her small, helpless son in her arms, her resolve weakened. *I should leave you here, but I cannot condemn you to death for the savagery of your father.*

The newborn never cried; he simply stared up into her eyes.

Do you sense that your silence is necessary for our survival?

She cleaned him as best she could and placed him at her breast to suckle. She lay back exhausted against the trunk and fell into a deep sleep.

Mother and child rested for a day before Willa forced herself to move on. She cut part of her cloak to make a swaddling blanket and a harness to bind the baby to the front of her body. Her foraging skills served her well, as she found what food she could along the way. Camouflaged and resting during the day, they traveled mostly by night, leading the horse through the dark shadows that provided safety and a shield against detection.

When she rested, she built no fire and held her son close to keep him warm. He gurgled as she nursed him and she rubbed his tiny cheek.

"You are a sweet boy, aren't you," she cooed. "My brave little warrior. I will get you home or die in the attempt."

Weeks later, when she crossed the open meadows of her territory and stood at the forest boundary of the Womara valley, tears welled up in her eyes. The sentries raced on horseback toward her as she lifted her son out of the harness.

"We are home, my little one," she said, bouncing him in her arms.

Escorted by scouts, they walked to the village center. Women stopped their work to stare at the strange woman—dirty, dressed in animal skins, and carrying a child. But then her mother recognized her, shouting out Willa's name from across the open space, and ran toward her with tears streaming down her face. Willa wanted to let her knees buckle but forced herself to stay standing when her mother and the other women surrounded her.

"You are not dead. You are not dead," her mother repeated over and over, as she cradled her face in her hands.

"Not dead," Willa answered, "Enslaved for this past year."

The women gasped at her words.

"Who took you?" a scout asked, glaring. "How did you escape?"

The young Womara leader, Dian, placed herself in their center. "Enough questions for now," she ordered the women. She turned to Willa and said, "I cannot begin to understand how much you have suffered. But you are safe now."

Willa's chin trembled, and the tears she had bravely held back spilled down her soiled face, leaving streaks upon her cheeks. Her mother hugged her tightly, causing her son to squirm in her arms as the women made their protective circle even tighter around her. Willa passed her child to her mother, and then from woman to woman.

She rested for days, safe in her home and with her mother by her side, as her swaddled son slept beside her.

"We searched for you for a month," her mother shared. "You never arrived at the village; no one had seen you. You disappeared without a trace." Her mother turned away to wipe a tear from her face. "It was with great anguish that we gave you up for dead."

Willa took her mother's hand. "It was a reckless move on my part, and the pride of a headstrong youth, not to take other women with me, thinking that I was above danger," she confessed.

When she was ready, Willa stood before Dian and the women's council to share all the facets of her abduction. Dian paced back and forth before her as Willa revealed the details of her rape and ongoing assaults.

"We shall avenge this barbarism!" Dian shouted.

"But I avenged it myself," Willa said. "I killed him at the first opportunity I had."

"Is it enough, this single act of retribution, or should we exact greater revenge for such a violation?" Dian argued. "There should be a price for such brutality enacted on any woman, let alone one of our own."

The women sat quietly, until an elder councilwoman rose. "You are our leader, Dian, but I caution restraint. The act of revenge on an entire tribe borders on brutality itself. I believe it is Willa's thoughts that matter here," she challenged.

The women all nodded and awaited Willa's words as she thought for a moment.

"I carried my freedom in my heart and lived daily with the conviction that this man would not break me, no matter how many times he violated my body." She looked around the room at the women standing before her. "Sometimes I wanted to give up," she said. "But when the right time appeared, I found my vengeance when I drove my knife into his heart. It was this man who needed to pay with his life, no other."

Dian looked to the council, who nodded in agreement. "So be it," Dian answered. "We shall respect your wishes."

"I would request something more of the council and my leader." Willa stepped closer to Dian. "It is tolerance that I ask for now. I would like for my son to be an accepted member of this clan. He is an innocent."

Dian placed a comforting hand upon Willa's shoulder and smiled. "Your son is one of us and will have many mothers."

That night at the evening fire, Dian stood before the women and announced, "Let us celebrate. May our hearts rejoice before the sacred fire at this joyous event, when we welcome our lost sister, Willa, back into our fold."

The women cheered, and Willa smiled shyly.

"It is a celebration, but one that might have had a very different outcome had it not been for Willa's courage. A very serious offense has been committed against a woman—a warrior. I sought the wisdom of the council today on how to avenge such an act, and we considered Willa's words and feelings about this atrocity."

"We seek death, do we not?" a warrior scout shouted.

"That was my sentiment," Dian answered, "until the council's advice tempered my impulse. Willa has made the final decision that we shall not seek retaliation against this tribe, because she achieved the vengeance she sought when she killed her violator."

Dian looked around at the faces of the women. "Nevertheless, I will share my feelings because my blood rises at the thought of men who think that women are property to do with what they wish, and who make us objects for their pleasure or sport."

"Aye!" the women yelled.

Dian continued, "Men will always use their physical prowess to force us into submission. We women have strong wills and must have the fortitude to fight back or outwit them, and to use our intuition to manipulate our enemy."

The circle of women grew quiet, listening intently.

"There was no shame in Willa's violation." Dian's voice rose as she strode before them. "For she survived, and each woman facing the same circumstances must survive as well. We must use our cunning to exact retribution, or man's aggressive nature may never be changed."

"The nature of men is set. It cannot be changed," a woman called out.

"Sadly, that may be so, but if men know there will be a price to pay for any act of violence, it might alter their behavior," Dian answered. "We bring men into our lives within the safety of our boundaries and under our rules. For the most part, these are good men who nurture and bring balance to us. We welcome them into our clan, but mankind is hostile outside our sanctuary, and that we cannot forget."

The women murmured in agreement.

"Only when a man forfeits his life will others rethink their acts. So let it be known that from this day forward, any man who enslaves or violates us will pay with his life, no matter how long it may take for us to find him," Dian concluded.

Willa looked at the women around the circle, glancing nervously at one another, as Dian continued. "I have searched my soul about what actions I would take under the same conditions that Willa endured. My act of revenge would be the same even if it resulted in my death. To avenge your violator's act could cost you your life, but men would then realize that we are willing to die for this ideal. If I did not survive, I would be comforted by the knowledge that my clan would seek justice on my behalf, no matter how long it might take to achieve. And my violator would never know another day of peace, wondering when we would come."

The women cheered.

"Do we stand united in a decree that any man who violates a Womara woman must pay with his own life?"

The women rapped their swords in unison on the ground.

"So be it!" Dian said.

The women solemnly placed their hands across their hearts in the final agreement.

Dian looked at Willa. "But let there also be a message of hope for us in that we ask something more of our sons, whom we raise among us and nurture toward a different way of being as they venture forth into the outside world. In a small way, we can pave a path for change through them. We will raise them to be better men."

Willa's heart swelled with pride at Dian's words. *I am still a warrior, one who has fought and lived, and I have not lost myself!*

Her mother, standing at her side, squeezed her arm. "Your survival has inspired this powerful new decree among our clan, Daughter, and your little one will grow to be a man who champions change."

Willa smiled down at her sleeping son in her arms. "He is my little warrior."

"What will you name him?" her mother asked.

"Randel—a name with dignity—and I will call him Rand."

11

THE VALLEY OF
THE WOMARA

The Womara pushed hard, putting distance between themselves and the band of men they had left in the meadow, but
Seanna could not shake off the unnerving sensation of having
faced down the intruders.

*I have grown slack living under the protection of James's city
walls, which can tame one's instincts to stay vigilant. A month of
scouting for the alliance would sharpen my senses again.*

Seanna's pulse quickened at the sight of the forest boundary.
She knew the sentries on lookout in the treetops would alert the
township to their arrival. As they approached the forest trails
leading to the interior, a small group of scouts waited to escort
them. Seanna dismounted and stood with her horse, patting her
neck.

"We are home," she said, as her mare tossed her head and
snorted.

Seanna looked up to view the canopy over her, inhaling the

air to catch the scent of the trees. She lowered her gaze to see the scouts grinning at her.

"Has the smell of the trees changed in your absence?" The lead scout smiled, before stepping forward to offer her forearm in an embrace. "It is good to have you home, Seanna."

The women dismounted and walked the final distance into the township, to welcome cries from the clan. Dian stood regally at the center, surrounded by the Womara council members.

I am glad to see you, Mother, Seanna thought. *My harsh words to you before my departure, challenging your decisions about the alliance, seem like a lifetime ago.*

She had spent many days watching and listening to James model his temperament as a king, and doing so had opened her to a greater understanding of the complexity of leadership. She had spent many hours in conversation about those challenges with James and believed she had gained a new maturity in any future discussions she had with her mother.

I have seen firsthand the abilities required to fulfill the role of a leader. As I have observed James struggling at times with those responsibilities, I have seen that a position of power can be a very lonely place.

Seanna crossed the distance of the square to stand before her mother and started to lower herself to one knee, but Dian would not allow it. Dian reached for her shoulders, drawing her close, and hugged her tightly, whispering in her ear, "Welcome back, my daughter. I am so grateful for your safe return."

When Dian released her, she reached out to lift Seanna's chin and look deeply into her eyes. As Seanna returned her regard unflinchingly, Dian said, "We received the message that you would return by sea and with an escort from your king's region."

"The king was considerate to send word. I did not want you to be concerned with my delay," Seanna answered.

"A light in your eyes seems to shine with glad tidings from this journey," Dian said.

Seanna nodded. "There is much to discuss."

Dian's eyes narrowed slightly as she continued to scrutinize her daughter. "Yet I sense a change in you, Seanna. I think many of the uncertainties you carried with you before you left have been answered."

Seanna gave her a slight smile and bowed her head.

Dian turned her attention to the other women with her. "Thealia, I am glad to see that you accompanied my daughter, but I am surprised to see you back so soon. Is all well at Lord Edmond's court?"

"Everything is fine, my lady," Thea answered. "In truth, I could not let Seanna leave without me. I thought she might have gotten soft in her time away and needed my escort." She glanced at Seanna and winked.

Dian only nodded, never changing her serious expression. "Good, then. Let us dine," she announced. "The council will join us, for we are eager to hear everything that has transpired in your absence."

Thea poked Seanna as they walked toward the hall. "Politics! Why can't we just head to the river to bathe?"

"Unfortunately, the river will have to wait," Seanna answered.

"I think from this point on, everything is about to change, Seanna," Thea said.

As they walked toward the hall, Seanna kept her thoughts to herself. *There was a time when serving as an alliance scout was my daily focus. Now I have returned under the flag of a king, escorted by his envoy, and Thea does not know how true her words are. Soon, indeed, everything will change.*

"What lies ahead for the future?" Thea asked.

"How can we know everything that will transpire? I will be relieved to leave those negotiations in the hands of the alliance council and my mother," Seanna answered.

Around the long oak dining table, Dian and the council members listened intently as Seanna shared the tale of her journey, beginning from the moment she arrived in James's homeland. Her mother and the council heeded her words closely as she spoke of the magnitude of the great city and the ports to the north.

"I have seen people and many new things that have exposed me to a new world," she said. "These experiences have opened to me the wonders of a new realm in ways that I could never have conceived."

"After your departure, your mother shared the discovery of the pass and the fact that the true objective of your journey was to return over the mountains to honor an oath to a prince whom you had saved," a councilwoman acknowledged.

"How fortunate you were to have earned his favor," another woman commented.

 Seanna stomach flinched at her hidden truth, but she offered only, "It is a great honor that he bestowed upon me in exchange for my help in returning his father's body to be buried among his ancestors."

"Do not be so humble," Dian said. "You saved a king's life. He repays a great debt."

"And one amply discharged," Seanna answered.

"Indeed," Dian said. "But your return is heralded, and you bring a king's envoy who will stand with you before the new alliance."

"Yes," Seanna answered, as she recounted Lord Orman's purpose in conveying parchments that outlined trade agreements representing the king's wishes.

"But the envoy does not accompany you here?" Dian asked.

Seanna stiffened a little against the back of her chair. "No, he is traveling to the court of Lord Arden as we speak, in the company of Lord Stuart."

Seanna felt her mother's eyes upon her. "Well, there must a reason for those actions, but tell us more of this king," Dian said.

Seanna hesitated for a moment, wishing to gauge her words and to conceal her personal emotions about James, and then said, "He is a young king, thrust into a new role by tragic circumstances. He possesses a progressive mindset and seeks expansion as he considers the value of opening a new trade route and the possibilities of uniting our different regions."

"You have alluded to these trade rights and the great prosperity of those who obtain them," a councilwoman said.

"Yes. In my opinion, they are priceless," Seanna answered.

"Does the king favor the alliance's suggested port of Lord Edmond?" Dian asked.

"We have discussed no other place," Seanna said, "and the king's mappers accompanied us to plot the best route and assess the port's viability."

Dian said, "I speak of it because, in your absence, I learned that Lord Warin, the southern clan leader, continues his arguments to build the port farther down the coast, in his region. He has continued to press alternatives to the discussions among the council."

"As I would expect," Seanna said. "It will not be well received that the Womara may have gained an advantage."

Dian sat thoughtfully before speaking. "We have not faced the alliance council yet, and your assurances are fragile until treaties are signed. The Womara could still encounter resistance from some of the clans and the council. Even with a strong advantage, we will gain nothing if we are not granted a seat on the alliance council," she concluded.

Dian settled back in her chair. "Is your favor with the king strong enough for you to stand alone against the alliance council?"

"Our alliance with the king will be very strong," Seanna answered.

"I hope so," Dian said. "I do not think that Lord Warin and his cronies will give up so easily when he learns of an advantage lost to his suggestions of obtaining a trading port. We may stand on the brink of a new day, my daughter, but I still think there is a fight ahead."

The woman at the table sounded their "ayes" as Thea glanced her way and lifted an eyebrow, signaling to Seanna a silent question about when she would share all her news. Seanna shook her head and continued to sit in silence.

With that, Thea stood up from the table and said, "My lady, if I may have your leave? I am weary from the journey."

"Of course, Thealia," Dian said. "It is late. Let us adjourn for this evening. We can continue our talks in the morning."

As the women rose to say their good nights, Dian told Seanna, "Let me have a few more moments of your time, Daughter."

As Seanna nodded her assent, Thea said, "I will see you both in the morning."

Seanna and Dian watched the women leave. Once they were alone in the chamber, Dian leaned across the table and said, "I will not keep you much longer, but I sense there is something that you are not telling me. You stayed a moon longer than our agreed-upon time. You must have seen some great advantage in remaining."

Seanna nodded.

"Are you afraid to speak the truth in the presence of our council?" Dian asked.

"Not afraid." Seanna rose to open the window, listening to the light rain that had begun to fall. When she turned back to face her mother, she said, "I was waiting for some privacy, for the details are intimate in the telling."

Dian leaned back in her chair, clasping her hands together and waiting patiently for a moment, before saying, "This is a matter of the heart, I suspect?"

"Yes, it is." Seanna could not repress her radiant smile as she announced, "I have fallen in love with the king."

Dian nodded knowingly. "Ah. So *this* is the change I sensed." She rose, walked to the window, and took both of Seanna's hands in hers. "You have given yourself freely to this man?"

"Yes, and he to me." Seanna flushed under her mother's gaze as Dian smiled at her. "And, new to that love, I hold it close to my heart right now. I do not wish to speak of auspicious beginnings and the great advantages of such a union."

Dian searched her face. "All right, Daughter," she said, as she reached out to touch Seanna's cheek gently, "But let me rejoice as a mother, for this new love completes you."

Seanna took a deep breath, feeling her fatigue. "Thank you, but in this moment I want to enjoy being home."

"I do not wish to press you this evening, Seanna, but I want to know more of this man who has won my daughter's love. We shall speak of it further tomorrow."

Seanna did not immediately return to her small home at the edge of the township. She wandered briefly through the market, watching the waning activities at the end of the day, and then walked to the river. As she made her way to the water's edge, she heard the patter of raindrops on the forest canopy. She disrobed, submerged herself in a hot pool, and lifted her face upward to feel the droplets on her skin. *I am tired, and I have had so little time to be alone. This feels wonderful.*

She sank more deeply into the pool, wishing to dispel from her thoughts her mother's darkened expression just before Seanna had left her company the previous night. "There is something else to discuss—something more pressing than the heart," Seanna had shared. "All the news is not as good as we would like. I did gain the king's assurance of a favorable outcome in the trade agreements, but his thoughts were much occupied with the news he received right before my departure."

"And what news is that?" Dian asked, furrowing her brow.

"His realm could be under threat. The king's cousin Thomas fled the city when it was discovered that James had survived the ambush that killed his father. Thomas has been declared guilty in fleeing but has now been given sanctuary across the sea, in the northern region of King Havlor. There, the king's spies report, he is attempting to gather strength in arms through uniting with barbarian tribes."

Dian had seated herself and leaned forward, hand on her chin. "Is there more?"

"James's kingdom speculates that his cousin's purpose is to claim the throne."

Dian's expression clouded. She rose and began pacing before Seanna. "That could be a looming threat that we do not want any part of."

"That is my fear also," Seanna answered. "But would not a threat to the city and the coastlines impact all regions? In time, would we not have to fight the same hordes?"

"Perhaps, but for now we cannot be drawn into a conflict," Dian said.

Seanna loosened her braid, freeing her hair to fan out in the water as she floated in the warm pool. She looked up into the night sky to view the faint flickering of distant stars through the breaking clouds as the storm passed overhead. An owl on a nearby tree limb called out as it shook the rain from its feathers, then launched itself from its perch in stealthy silence, flying in the direction of an answering hoot across the forest.

Seanna's thoughts turned to James. *I miss you, my love.*

When she sat up, water droplets trickled down between her breasts and her skin tingled as she remembered James's eyes upon her the first night after their lovemaking, as she had risen from bathing herself in the river while he waited on the bank. Seanna ran her hands down her body now, touching herself.

I have never known such ecstasy as I did when he embraced me, drawing me down into the stream as the water caressed our movements and we became one with the river.

The following morning, Seanna rose early, summoned to meet her mother in Dian's private quarters. A mist from the previous night's rain still clung to the treetops in white shrouds. Large black ravens clinging to the branches stood out in sharp contrast, crying out their warnings when she passed. She was refreshed and clearheaded from a good night's sleep in her own bed, and ready to answer the questions that she knew were to come.

What I shared with my mother last night tempers our triumph, but I needed to reveal what I knew of James's threat from his cousin. However, I hope she will not reveal to the others my private feelings for James.

She paused before Dian's chamber door, resolving, *I will not allow my mother to use our love as a bargaining piece.*

The council and Dian stood waiting in her mother's chambers, viewing several maps spread out on the table. Dian summoned her closer. "I have shared some of your disclosures from last evening with the council. Show me what you know of this coastline," she ordered.

For the next several hours, Seanna detailed all that she recalled about the geography of the region. Dian and the council sat quietly, staring intently at the maps, until her mother broke the silence: "There is great vulnerability along these uncharted parts of the king's coast."

Seanna nodded. "I conveyed that fact to him. When I first discovered the pass and crossed over to discover his ambushed camp. I knew from the tracks of his father's assailants that they had traveled from this part of the coast inland, to lie in wait for the king's party."

Seanna stiffened when Dian asked, "And the pass between the mountains. Who knows?"

"The king and all the men who accompanied him to retrieve his father's body. There were trackers among them who could surmise from my descent that I had not traveled a coastal route. It served no purpose to disguise from which direction I had come. For a full year, the king has held this secret about the pass. It was his pledge to me."

"But it is now known. Are we vulnerable?" Dian asked.

"To those who wish an arduous journey from the valleys below, an extreme climb to the peaks, and an equally dangerous descent to the other side, maybe so. But if an invasion is the objective of the king's cousin, all regions would be more vulnerable by sea," Seanna concluded.

As the councilwomen cast wary glances at her mother, Dian asked, "What this king might demand in support is the pressing question. Did this Lord Orman who accompanied you stipulate that we must declare allegiance to the king before we sign any trade agreement?"

"No, he did not, and the king, whom I have come to know, would not require such conditions. I believe that his directive to Lord Orman was to negotiate terms in regard to trade only."

"It appears that you have indeed made inroads and gained the confidence of the king," a councilwoman said.

"You have done well," another offered.

Seanna nodded her thanks but was not prepared for the next question: "This new king is unmarried, is he not? Does he seek a marriage alliance that could offer him a valuable layer of protection outside his region and solidify his allies?"

Seanna looked at her mother, who stood watching her in

silence. "That does not concern us," Dian retorted. "We must concentrate on the task before us first, and hold the alliance council to their assurance of our inclusion. Then we shall move to secure a treaty of trade and add our pledge to build the port in Lord Edmond's region. Tomorrow we depart for Lord Arden's court."

When the council had gone, Seanna stood alone with her mother. "I thank you for not breaking my confidence," she said.

"How long do you think you can hold your feelings in secret? It is only a matter of time before your truth emerges."

Seanna nodded. "I suppose I cling to the illusion that our love will change nothing. For now, I do not wish to view that illusion differently."

"Did you reveal to James that your father is Lord Arden?"

"No," Seanna answered quickly.

"And why not, Daughter?"

"You said that was my secret to hold. I am not sure that I have reconciled myself to its truth yet, and I could not find an appropriate time to share this new knowledge with the king."

"As your father's heir, the region could be a major strategic advantage for this king," Dian said. "You speak of trust with this man to whom you have declared your love, but you held back?"

Seanna shrugged. "I don't know why. I followed my instincts."

Dian nodded. "You have grown wiser in these past months, my daughter, and have learned to temper your judgments."

"I need no temperance with James," Seanna replied. "But there are others whom I do not trust."

"I agree. There is much work to be done to lay the groundwork for these negotiations, without the complications of love. Who knows of this union?" she pressed.

"Thea and the envoy Lord Orman," Seanna answered. "Lord

Orman does not approve and, in his own words to me, stated he would rather have the king married in an alliance of merit."

"Orman travels ahead with Stuart to Arden's court, and I will trust your instincts that he is no friend to our cause," Dian reflected.

"There is a divisive undercurrent to everything he proposes," Seanna said.

"Do you think that Stuart will keep a watchful eye on him?"

"Yes," Seanna answered. "But I was able to spend only a brief amount of time in the counsel of Lord Edmond and Stuart. It is difficult to disguise my mistrust of Lord Orman, but I should have spoken more candidly to Stuart of my concerns."

"Stuart is no fool," Dian said.

Seanna nodded. "But Orman is honey-tongued and speaks powerfully of unity and new beginnings. It is not possible to know what lies beneath his thoughts. Maybe I owe him the benefit of acting for the good of all in these days ahead?"

"Do not second-guess yourself, Seanna. Remember, the nature of a fox does not change, even though he will eat the food offered from your hand. Enjoy your remaining hours at home, for we leave at dawn tomorrow."

12

DANCE OF FIRE

Seanna left her mother's chambers at midday and walked to the forest meadow, wanting some solitude and a respite from her thoughts concerning the direction of her conversations with Dian and other councilwomen.

We leave soon for Lord Arden's region, and I will return to the fray of the politics of men. I hoped for a little more time before our departure tomorrow morning, but it was naive to wish to defer the commencement of actions and their outcomes.

She left the path to stand at the edge of a large meadow and watched the long grasses undulating in the soft breezes. Across the field stood her favorite tree, a majestic oak with large, twisted limbs, which dominated the surrounding foliage and had been her touchstone since her childhood.

She crossed the meadow, running her fingertips over the tips of the dry grass stalks as she inhaled their scent, and stood before her tree. *How long have you stood silently waiting, my old friend, knowing I will always return?*

She reached out and lovingly rubbed her hand along the trunk; the bark was rough to her touch. *Your skin is as lined and ridged as our old healer's face—both of you wear your visage as an emblem of a life long lived.*

She leaned back to look up into the canopy and grabbed a lower branch, pulled herself onto it, and continued to climb high to her favorite spot, where she could lean back into a bend that cradled her body. The tree's giant branches surrounded her, and the camouflage of leaves provided the haven she sought as she nestled her body closer into the trunk. *Have I not drawn some of my wisdom and clarity from the strength of your limbs?*

She watched the wind ripple across the grasses again as she began to sort through her muddled mind to unravel all the conversations that had taken place over the past several days. In spite of her mother's dark predictions concerning the entanglement of politics and the obligations that Seanna's new bond with James might imply, it was the words Seanna had exchanged with Thea on their journey home that disturbed her most.

When they had sat together around their campfire that night in the darkened forest, Thea had posed a question about Stuart that expressed Seanna's secret worries about James, too. It was not that Thea questioned her commitment to and love for Stuart; it was a deeper inquiry that troubled her: "We Womara have no masters. Can the constraints of love and duty be too great? How can we be free and love at the same time?"

Her mother had expressed her happiness for Seanna's love of James but had cast a shadow over it by emphasizing the obligations that it might carry, magnifying the challenges of mixing love and politics. Seanna had not shared with Thea or Dian her lingering concern about those words, and about balancing two lives as different as hers and James's. Before she had departed for her home, neither she nor James had proposed a vision of their future; she speculated that he held back as much as she from posing as-yet-unanswerable questions: *Will the divide of time and distance between us be too great?* And, even more pressing: *Now that I am home again within my forest, will my resolve to depart weaken?*

Seanna pressed herself against her tree, wrapping her arms around her knees and seeing James's shining face before her in her mind's eye. *How could I ever envision not returning to him?*

She hugged herself even more tightly to contain the quickening of her heartbeat at the thought of their first night together, when James had taken her to his forest. She closed her eyes to relive the memory, seeing herself standing before the inert logs of the ritual fire that he had constructed. Her chest tightened as she remembered how she had misunderstood the intent of his gesture.

I thought he mocked our sacred ritual. But how quickly my anger turned to elation when he declared his love. He enveloped me in his embrace, and it was hard to break away from his arms to return to the cottage and prepare myself as he lit the fire.

She smiled, remembering how shy she had felt inside the cottage, wondering, *What do I do?*

Upon the floor was the pack from her horse; it contained a pale green silk wrap that was a gift from her mother, purchased in the marketplace the day before. She removed her scout clothes and wrapped the cloth around her body, enjoying the softness against her skin and feeling her nakedness accentuated through the thin fabric. She loosened her braid and let her hair fall free down her back. *My heart was beating so hard, and I could not control my trembling.*

When she left the cottage, she had to breathe deeply to steady her senses. The night air was warm against her skin, and in the distance, she could see the glow of burning logs as she walked the path toward the fire.

She lingered at the edge of the trail to watch James. He stood waiting, and the flames behind him created a glowing silhouette. His torso was bare, with dark chest hair the same color as his head. She admired his well-formed body, with a narrow waist and toned muscles.

How handsome he is! she thought. *Have I conjured from the deepest recesses of my mind all that I find desirable in a man and summoned him to me here, in the flesh?*

As she stepped out from the shadows of the trees, moving toward James, she watched his eyes follow her. When she stopped before him, he reached out and took her hands. His words stirred her heart. "Seanna, you are so beautiful," he said as he drew her to him and enfolded her in his arms.

I felt my body tremble against his.

"My love, my love," he whispered over and over, holding her until she calmed. When she looked up at him, he kissed her deeply, seeking her tongue with his. He ran his hands down her arms and then lightly over her breasts, causing her to shiver.

She rested her hands on his chest, and he watched her as she traced the line of hair between his breasts with her finger, following the soft down to the center of his abdomen and disappearing below his breeches. He pulled her closer, and she felt his hardened manhood against her.

James took her hand, leading her into the trees and to a bed of soft ferns. Underneath the forest canopy, the moon filtered through the leaves and softly illuminated the grasses as he slowly unwrapped the cloth that bound her body. He stepped back to view her, smiling as he silently moved his eyes over her naked form. "Your skin glows from the light of the moon," he said.

I was shy with his eyes upon me, but I surprised him with my next words:

"I have never had a man look at me the way you are seeing me now."

James stepped closer to her. "You have not known a man before me?" he asked. "I just assumed . . ."

"Do not give me false virtue," she said. "I did try, only to give up. I wasn't ready. I have no experience with men, but I come to you because I want to. It is my choice to whom I give myself, and I have chosen you."

"Come here," James said. He took her hands, pressed her naked body against his, and then lowered her onto the cloth upon the ground.

I remember so vividly the softness of the cloth and the musky smell of the earth and ferns around me, Seanna reflected.

James caressed her entire body then, watching her closely as she lay with her arms resting above her. His fingers stroked her thighs, and then he gently placed one hand upon her mound and touched the soft folds of the skin there, making her gasp and arch her back against the pressure.

She placed her hand on top of his. "Don't stop," she said. "I like that."

James leaned over to kiss her, and she rose up to reach his mouth, eager to feel his lips on hers as she sought the feel of his soft tongue. He moved his lips to her breasts, kissing each one, and, breathing deeply, she thought she would not be able to contain herself. James gently opened her legs, running his hands again down her inner thighs and making her tremble. He approached her with caution, but she lifted her legs and wrapped them around him tightly, urging him to enter her fully.

I felt a brief moment of pain.

James stopped and steadied himself before moving slowly upon her. As rising ecstasy filled her body, she moved with him. He ran his hands under her buttocks, lifting her higher, and she felt him move more deeply into her as they groaned in unison.

All my senses rose to one point, and I abandoned the world. I never imagined myself moaning out loud as I did. James, knowing that he had satisfied me, quickened his movements unconstrained, shuddering at his release and calling out my name.

In the tree, Seanna shifted her position, feeling arousal rise in her body as she remembered their passion. She watched a small bird flit among the branches and smiled at the thought of the utter contentment she had felt after their joining. Her entire body tingling, she had lain on her side, gazing at James, who was on his back, looking into the sky.

He reached over and touched her face. "It is the most beautiful night, is it not?" he asked.

Seanna sat up and smiled down at him. "When you asked me here to your special place, I never imagined that this was what would happen."

"I wanted it to happen much sooner than this," he said, stroking her arm. "It was Cedmon who helped me find my courage."

"How did he help you?" Seanna asked.

"He made me see that if you left and I never knew how you felt, I would regret it always."

"What if I had not returned your affections?"

"It still would have been better to know that I tried than to live my life wondering. It took no courage to act when I imagined a life without you."

"And now you have me," Seanna teased him.

"Yes, I do." He smiled, touching her hair. "I will never forget you in this moment, with the moonlight shining on your wild hair and the beauty of your body."

"I am taking this body to the river to wash," she said, laughing as she made her way to the water.

James's eyes upon her in the half-light were luminous as she rose from the river. He gathered her to him once more, pressing his bare chest against hers to warm her cold skin with his body, and kissed her passionately.

Seanna sighed, feeling the ache of wanting him. *These musings are not helping to quiet my thoughts!* she realized, as she heard Thea call her name from across the meadow.

13

THE NEW WARRIORS

Thea strode across the meadow while Seanna remained sitting quietly in the top of her tree. She stopped at the base of the trunk.

"Do you think that you can hide from me for the entire day?" Thea shouted up to her.

"I thought I would try," Seanna said, laughing. "But I will come down now." She descended the limbs of the tree and jumped the last several feet to the ground.

"What were you doing up there?" Thea smiled mischievously. "I have found you because there is someone here who wants to see you."

Seanna raised an eyebrow as Thea signaled for her to follow. They walked a well-worn path that led to the Womara training area. When they entered, Seanna stood for a moment, looking around the empty grounds, before she saw Gareth, her alliance scout companion, standing at the far side with his arms crossed over his chest, grinning broadly at her.

Seanna laughed in delight as Gareth strode across the space to grab her forearm. "Well, here you are at last, and I hear you have returned a hero, if the stories are true."

"What do they say?" Seanna asked.

"That you journeyed over a mountain pass to the northern continent and saved a king."

"He wasn't a king when I found him, only a prince," Seanna said.

Gareth smirked. "Well, we have some stories to catch up on, do we not?"

"Yes, but what are you doing here?"

"Shortly after you left, I was sent, at Lord Arden's behest, to seek additional Womara warriors to serve the alliance as scouts. Lord Arden has wisely determined that the alliance needs to extend our numbers and our reach. I have been a guest of your mother for the past several weeks."

"A guest of my mother!" Seanna laughed again. "And how have you found your time here, as well as her company?"

"We have had several hours of fascinating conversations over a few shared meals. I must say that her questions and observations about the alliance and its politics are most astute." He gave Seanna a familiar sideways grin, but his expression grew serious as he continued. "But let me say that your home is everything that you have described to me, and being here has been an illuminating experience."

"Ah, my old friend—you may finally come to understand me," Seanna jested. "And have you recruited any good candidates among our warriors?"

"Several. There are some very impressive fighters here," Gareth replied.

Seanna glanced across the grounds at the four young Womara warriors waiting silently with Willa, their trainer. All the women stood straighter as Gareth and Seanna walked toward them, and Willa stepped forward, bowing to Seanna with her hand over her heart.

"It is a blessing that you returned safely, Seanna," she said.

"Thank you, Willa. And I understand that you have had the pleasure of spending time with Gareth, my alliance commander."

"That sounds so formal." Gareth laughed.

Willa glanced at Gareth shyly. "Yes, we have worked together over these past weeks to select the candidates who will compete in the alliance trials."

Seanna surveyed the young women. They ranged in age from fifteen to seventeen years; each was chosen for her proficiency in many areas of fighting. "What competencies for the trials are you demonstrating today?" she asked.

"No trials here," Gareth answered. "These women do not need to earn their place at this level. I have the authority to select the women who will travel back with me to Lord Arden's township to compete with others from the regions' clans as potential alliance scouts."

"When do you leave?" Seanna asked.

"When you do," Gareth answered. "Your mother requires an escort of warriors to accompany her, including these young women as her bodyguards."

Seanna smiled at the candidates, knowing the honor bestowed upon them.

Gareth glanced back at the warrior recruits and said, "The training skill I have found most impressive is the Womara's ability to use the objects in their surroundings for evasive techniques, as well as the agility those moves require."

Seanna nodded as Gareth continued, "Willa has informed me that this aspect of training exists in the everyday play and games of the Womara children."

"Yes, we start young," Seanna said.

"That is the very factor that makes your fighting techniques unconventional and unique—agility and aerobatics combine into fluid movement. I doubt that a man could learn how to execute these moves as effortlessly as these women," Gareth said.

"Our young men can," Seanna said. "Those who are raised among us have the same skills. Let me watch," she added, as Willa signaled to the women to take their positions. They stood in twos, each holding a sword, facing off. At Gareth's signal, they took off in a full run across the arena, as one pursued the other. Each young girl being chased used an evasive maneuver to catapult off the closest object and somersault over her pursuer, landing directly behind her and delivering a striking blow to her attacker's back.

Seanna turned to Gareth. "Impressive, is it not? As you can see, the aerobatics included in their training since they were children have many advantages in a surprise or evasive assault."

Gareth added, "Not only that, but these women have led me deep into the woods. I tried to follow as they jumped across small gorges and ran along logs that crossed rushing streams, but I hesitated. When they ran ahead, I often passed them on trails, unable to detect their presence because they were so well camouflaged in the nature surrounding them."

"An important aspect of our defense if our forests are ever penetrated," Seanna offered.

Gareth nodded. "I have also seen these women jump onto tree limbs with bows on their backs, expending almost no effort, and swing themselves up to the treetops in seconds. I will confess that my first impulse was to judge as cowardly this act of not facing their foe."

"But, again, it is an effective defense for us," Seanna said.

"Yes, for I have witnessed their climbing speed and their ability to shoot, with deadly accuracy and within seconds, from high in the tree limbs. I have come to appreciate that you know how to use your surroundings for survival. That is a lesson well learned for anyone," Gareth concluded.

Seanna nodded. "There is no winning in death."

Gareth signaled for the women to go again, and Seanna watched as a young warrior named Ava leaped off a tree trunk, slightly off-center, and threw herself sideways, almost suspended for a moment in slow motion, then corrected her position midair to land directly behind her opponent.

I have always admired her, Seanna thought. *She is a fierce fighter. But she has a maturity and a balanced temperament that are beyond her age—all of which she will need if she is to become a scout for the alliance.*

As if reading her thoughts, Gareth commented, "It is Ava who is most impressive. There are not many who would survive any weapon thrown from her hand."

Willa added, "Yes, she is deadly with the javelin but prefers the longbow, which acts as an extension of her arm and increases the distance of her throw. I have seen her cast while riding astride a fully galloping horse and hit her target almost every time."

"She is also a master with horses," Seanna said.

"Also true," Willa answered. "She is able to control the movements of the animal expertly using pressure from her knees. That allows her to keep her arms and hands free to shoot her bow or throw her javelin. I think she will make an excellent alliance scout—a special honor for any warrior now that you, Seanna, have paved the way for other women."

Seanna smiled warmly at her praise. "But she has bloomed under your tutelage, Willa."

"The alliance trials will be challenge enough, but some of the women want a chance to fight raiders, as I overheard one young Womara confide to another," Willa said.

"Are they concerned about the prospect of living among the townships of men?" Seanna asked. "It is certainly a valuable opportunity to serve in the alliance, but leaving poses a different type of challenge. I know how I felt away from my home."

She added silently to herself, *Willa's son, Rand, has been an alliance warrior for two years now. I wonder if that influenced Ava's decision to compete in the trials.*

Ava and Rand had been childhood playmates and later training warriors, often paired because of their size and strength. Ava was tall, with pale-colored hair and blue eyes, in contrast with Rand's dark and brooding good looks. He was strong and muscled, with the physique of his father's nomadic people, but his penetrating gaze carried the intensity of one raised as a Womara.

At puberty, all young men left the Womara forests to live outside their mothers' community. Some boys returned to the villages and towns of their fathers. Others, with no known father, choose to serve as soldiers in a certain clan leader's territory or apprentice in a particular trade.

Rand had chosen Lord Arden's region, wishing to be part of the new and progressive alliance and the developing unity of clans. Seanna knew he had returned several moons ago to visit his mother. He and Ava had been seen at the full-moon fire and then riding together the following day. *They are well-suited if they are mated*, Seanna thought.

Seanna turned to Gareth and Willa. "They are warriors of worth, but they need more than the skills of fighting. They will find a callous world outside the realm of the Womara, among the clans of men."

"I agree," Gareth said. "That is why they will all continue their training among our alliance fighters."

Seanna raised her eyebrows in surprise. "An opportunity that I was not afforded," she said.

"No," Gareth replied. "For we never expected you to pass the trials. You surprised us all."

After Gareth dismissed the young women, Seanna turned to Willa. "You should be proud. They are as prepared as much as they can be, but do not underestimate the contempt of those outside our clan—there are many who wish to see us fail."

"I know," Willa said. "You are right that it will be a harsh reality to leave this haven that is our way of life. Our young men provide some contrast in training, but these youth have grown up together and know each other's ways too well."

"The divergence outside your forest will deepen their training," Gareth said.

"It is necessary for them to grow as fighters. I know only too well the brutality of the outside world of men and the threat of danger they pose," Willa said. Seanna noticed her flushing at her own reference to her abduction.

When Gareth asked, "What do you speak of?" Seanna quickly changed the topic: "And what of your Rand? How does he fare in service to Lord Arden?"

Willa beamed. "He is well and, I am proud to say, a valued addition to the alliance warriors."

"He is one of the best new fighters that we have," Gareth added.

Seanna sighed. "Why do I suddenly feel so old?" As they all laughed, she teased Gareth: "Though I may still have some more tricks to teach you."

"How so?"

"In the king's region, I was able to observe his guards' fighting techniques and their rigidity in holding to that conventionality. It reinforced my belief that adaptability should be at the core of any battle strategy."

"Yes, but adaptability is something to be studied and learned," Gareth said.

"True, that is why we should continue to change."

"Does that apply to all women and to children as well?" Gareth asked, with a smile.

"Why not?" Seanna replied. "All of the children above age five in my clan can take out your eye with a slingshot and an acorn."

"And under five?" Gareth asked.

"They gather the acorns." Seanna laughed, then said, "I jest, but in seriousness I cannot share yet what might transpire when I journey to Lord Arden's region to meet the alliance. A great change could come soon."

"A change for the better, I hope," Gareth said.

"The value of the alliance to our region will require openness to other cultures that could soon be a part of the new trading port. We must be willing to accommodate new ideas. I was humbled to realize what a small part we play in the vast areas of lands that exist," Seanna continued.

"I agree that the strength of our people lies in our ability to change with these new times," Willa offered.

"I think this great city must be something to see," Gareth answered. "And you, Willa?"

Willa's eyes darted to Gareth. "My world will not extend far beyond this forest," she answered haltingly.

Seanna saw that Willa flushed at his attention, as Gareth fumbled: "At least, I am glad that you have agreed to accompany us to Arden's court with the new warriors."

"It will be an opportunity to see my son and also to make sure my young women are settled in," Willa answered.

"Of course," Gareth replied.

Seanna watched her two friends, gauging their words. *Is this flirtation? I never thought I would witness Gareth showing attention to any woman, or Willa returning it in kind to any man, so dark have been her wounds.* She smiled to herself as she added, *Hasn't my intuition always told me that one day you would live among us, Gareth?*

14

THE WOMARA ARRIVE

O rman walked the wooden ramparts that encircled the township of Lord Arden as he observed the landscape beyond the walls. The sun hung high on the horizon, and the sky was brilliantly clear. He paused to appreciate the flush of colors in the surrounding countryside, letting his eyes follow the road that led away from the main gate for a mile and then disappeared into the forests, merging with paths that led to the other, smaller surrounding villages.

This new region has a primitive natural beauty that still presses back against the man-made boundaries of the township, and no brick or stone within miles of anyone's gaze. The vision evokes a distant memory of the earlier times of my city and the changes that progress inevitably brings.

Orman returned to his leisurely stroll, enjoying the highest viewpoints of the township and letting his thoughts wander. He had scarcely had a moment to himself since he had departed the coast with Lord Stuart and his accompanying entourage; eager clansmen had been vying constantly for his ear, always pursuing him for discussion. Upon his arrival in Lord Arden's region, the alliance council members had pressed him to begin the implementation of their talks. He had grown tired of the many tedious moments when he needed to pull himself away from private conversations initiated by over-eager clansmen. *These men certainly lack the sophistication and the protocol of a king's council*, he thought.

The exception to his observations was Lord Arden, who needed no introduction when Orman entered his hall for their first meeting. Lord Arden's presence dominated the room, radiating the self-awareness of a man distinguished by his strength of character. Not only was he imposing in stature, but he also emanated the confidence of a leader meeting an equal when Orman stood before him. Arden stared him directly in the eye, not like the darting looks of the lower lords that revealed their unconscious belief that they were lesser in social ranking. Arden's eyes shone with a piercing directness that burned with inner passion.

I like him, Orman thought.

In the days that followed, as he mingled among the councilmen, Orman heard narratives about Arden's ability to hear and balance the needs of all. Other leaders praised his capacity to unite the disparate clans under a shared vision that they could develop trade ports that would benefit everyone. He had earned his place as the elected leader of the alliance council based on the respect he had garnered over years.

Orman observed him from across the room, thinking, *A noble endeavor, this vision of prosperity for all, and so far I have not been able to detect any character flaws that counter it. He appears to be a rare man, one of the caliber of my own king, whom I respected but still plotted to dethrone. There must be something in the moral fabric of these men that ultimately gives me satisfaction to watch them fail.*

Over the past several days, Lord Arden had skillfully distilled all the information that he and the mappers could convey to the council. Orman watched Arden as he listened with his full attention to the voices of the councilmen and often redirected an impatient group of them, unaccustomed to cooperation, as a master tutor might control a room of disruptive students. Arden also held fast to his refusal to begin any formal discussions without the Womara present, no matter how eager the men were.

Lord Arden and the Womara's history is long and intertwined. I must gather as much information as I can about the origins of their bond.

Orman found that many of the clansmen on the council viewed the female clan favorably. It was the disruptive voice of Lord Warin and the dissenting votes of the southern clans that had cost the Womara a place in the newly formed alliance, and a seat at the alliance council's table.

Once the votes had been cast against her clan, Seanna had disrupted the outcome of the council vote by announcing the discovery of a mountain pass over the peaks that separated their northern region from the continent beyond. She had announced she would depart in few days for a secret reunion with James, now the king, whom she had recused from certain death.

Her veiled warning to the council implied that if she did not have their support when she left, she would represent only the best interests of her clan in any diplomatic negotiations that might transpire, including those about whether a trade agreement was possible, and would thereby disrupt the council's own trade aspirations and its plans for building a port.

Seanna challenged these councilmen and revealed the secret pass and her story about rescuing a prince to gain leverage. I would not have thought her capable of such a manipulation, but she clearly fights back when her passions are inflamed. I find it most disturbing that she and James kept this rendezvous secret for almost a year, and that the king was complicit in that knowledge all along.

Several of the council members pressed Orman privately about Seanna's present disposition, assuming that he would have better insight because she had spent time in his city and they had traveled together to this region. The men asked whether she harbored any resentment about the Womara's rebuffed bid for a council seat. Orman found that he could not answer the inquiries honestly, for Seanna held her emotions closer than any woman he had ever known, and in truth he knew she would never confide in him about even the simplest of sentiments.

Seanna is not even aware of the power she may hold over the council, or of how willing they may be to placate her.

The men had expressed candidly to Orman their hope that they had not alienated her goodwill, now that she had returned successfully from her journey to restore a dead king to his son. *Two-faced, all of you*, he bristled, *in now wishing to share in the favor the king has bestowed on her.*

Of more concern, they appeared ready to grant the Womara a place in the council. *There is a worthy game of chess to be played using these men's emotions. No one seems to know of her romance with the king. If they did, how would that change their view of her?*

He had also learned that Stuart, in defiance of the council, had staked his position beside Seanna by speaking out in the Womara's favor. His wish to develop the port in his township appeared to be based on his loyalty to her alone. It would have been a greater risk for Stuart to voice his opposition covertly. His words could have alienated the support of the council and incurred his father's wrath for speaking without his consent. The great gamble rested on Seanna's journey and on the hope that her reunion with the king would be fruitful in establishing trade ties.

But do Lord Arden and Stuart already know of her union with James? If so, how could that tilt the negotiations?

Orman observed that the two lords often sought each other's council during their frequent private conversations. Stuart appeared to be a younger version of Lord Arden; though he was untested in conflict, the former had the makings of a strong leader and seemed to possess the even temperament and visionary scope of Lord Arden. Together, they would make a powerful union.

The only chess piece missing is the leader of the Womara, Dian, and the unanswered question of where she will move on this board of power.

Orman had reached the far end of the walkway, where he paused. He was pleased that the undertone of dissent that his spies had initially reported to him existed as a fact. He had discovered that opposition from the southern region and its clan leader, Lord Warin, still smoldered.

On the first day of Orman's arrival, following his introductions to the councilmen, Lord Warin had approached him. A burly and unkempt man, he boasted that he was the leader of the second-largest region in the realm, and that his coastal clan was closest in proximity to Lord Edmond.

Warin lacked subtlety and was quick to interject that there were other port options to consider, and that his length of coast was just as suitable a site for a trading port. He appeared to be in cooperation with the new alliance but revealed to Orman that the council's discussion about the port had been contentious. Seanna's proposed rendezvous with Prince James had only further complicated the decision.

I found his openness to voice a dissenting opinion exactly what I had sought, Orman reflected, *but I was averse to his abject narcissism and ambition, which appeared to be the core of his willingness to disrupt. I suspect that I have not heard the last from this man; there is something more he wants from me, and he will no doubt press his interests.*

Echoing horns in the distance, announcing the arrival of the Womara, cut short Orman's thoughts.

So, they come. He smiled as he made his way to the township's meeting hall.

Orman waited at Lord Arden's side and watched him rise from his seat as the doors of the long hall opened. Brilliant midafternoon light streamed through the entrance, momentarily obscuring the emerging figures.

Twenty Womara women advanced toward him. Orman assumed the woman leading the group to be Dian. She was flanked by Seanna and Thea, whom he knew. Four well-armed, younger Womara women walked directly behind Dian, and the remaining women followed. Orman noted that the room had gone silent and that every man had turned with a curious stare to watch the female clan walking the length of the hall.

The women were dressed for travel and wore fitted vests of leather or linen, over tunics and skirts that fell to their thighs or knees. Ornately designed buckles fastened the belts at their waists.

The colors of their clothes reminded Orman of the changing tones of the forest he had observed earlier that day: light browns and greens, russets and reds, and the yellow gold of Dian's tunic.

Simple brooches of bronze or silver fastened their woolen cloaks around their shoulders, and Dian's cloak was lined with animal fur. Some of their coverings bore intricate woven patterns, reminding Orman that the Womara women were renowned for their weaving abilities and considered master artisans. Other garments bore runic symbols on the simple trim around the neckline.

Their hair was elaborately plaited and bound by leather ties or simple clasps. The long, single braids that hung at their temples were intertwined with small colored beads or carved bone. Dian's hair was coiled elegantly around her head, but a portion of her tresses flowed free to her mid-back.

All of the women carried some type of weapon, such as a knife or a short sword, in their belt. Others carried a long sword at their side, their hands still on the hilt, and a bow on their back.

Well-armed and strong-willed was the impression that crossed Orman's mind.

Dian stopped before the platform where Lord Arden stood waiting. She bowed her head, one hand placed on her heart, but did not kneel, as would have been the custom of a clansman greeting him.

"Lord Arden, it is an honor to see you again. It has been too long since our last meeting."

"Indeed it has, Dian of the Womara. We welcome you."

The room remained quiet as the men stood transfixed. Arden stared at Dian's face for several seconds before he broke the stillness and turned to his men. "Lords of the council, let me introduce Dian, clan leader of the Womara."

Dian turned to face the room and bowed before them. "My lords, it is an honor." Gesturing toward Seanna, she added, "Please allow me to introduce my daughter, Seanna, to those who do not know her."

Some of the men in the group bowed their heads in recognition.

Arden moved aside as Stuart stepped forward and bowed. "Lady Dian."

"Lord Stuart," Dian said.

Arden gestured at Orman and said, "You have not had the pleasure of meeting Lord Orman, envoy to King James, of the northern continent of our region and the city of Bathemor."

Orman stepped forward, bowing low as Dian stepped toward him and said, "Lord Orman, it is a pleasure. I have heard much about you from my daughter." Her smile was gracious as he felt her gaze linger on his face.

"The pleasure is mine, Lady Dian. It is an honor to be invited to this great region as a representative of King James. We cannot express the depth of our people's gratitude for your daughter's courage in the rescue of our sovereign."

My words are sincere, Orman thought. *I have been truly curious to meet this woman. Are the attributes of strength that the daughter embodies borne from her mother?*

Dian tipped her head slightly, acknowledging the compliment.

Orman took advantage of his proximity to Dian to view her closely. As she stood before him, he could not help but recognize how handsome a woman she was. Her hair, pulled away from her face, exposed her fine features and long neck, and he could see where Seanna had acquired her beauty. Her emerald-green eyes were the exact color of her daughter's. Her simple gold earrings caught the light and matched the color of her tunic.

Her look is not directly challenging but discomfiting nonetheless. Her beauty aside, I cannot deny that her entrance into the hall was an impressive sight. She is a most potent figure.

Arden proceeded with his introductions of the leaders of the various regions that comprised the alliance council. Orman watched them circulate around the room as Dian stopped before each man to personally acknowledge him. She lingered on Lord Warin longer, and Orman noted that the lord shifted his stance uncomfortably under her gaze.

The remaining women, including Seanna and Thea, had stood at unflinching attention during the introductions, until Arden announced, "You have all had a long journey. The servants will settle you in your quarters before we dine. Let us have a toast to begin this auspicious gathering. This evening we will get to know one another better, and tomorrow we can begin our talks in earnest."

The clansmen murmured among themselves as Arden signaled to his servants to pour the wine.

A nod of Dian's head released her warriors, and the scouts relaxed their grip on their swords while the servants filled everyone's glasses. Orman observed that the younger warrior women and one older woman who stood with them remained on guard and declined the drink; *these must be Dian's bodyguards.*

Warin crossed the room to place himself at Lord Orman's side. In a low voice, he said, "So, now you have met the leader of the Womara."

Orman nodded and asked, "And what of you, Lord Warin? What are your initial perceptions?"

"In truth, I have never met Dian," Warin answered. "Nor did I have much interest in doing so before this day." Warin leaned in closer to Orman and smirked. "Do not be swayed by the power of their presence. They are still only women. They have been afforded equal status merely because they call themselves warriors."

Orman said, stoking Warin's rancor, "Why not warriors, Lord Warin? I have witnessed the fighting skills of one woman. It is prudent not to underestimate their collective prowess if she accurately represents their skills."

One cannot forget that they are warriors first! The daughter, Seanna, could be judged as politically naive and is finding her balance between warrior and leader, but the mother knows exactly the range of her power and should not be dismissed so lightly.

Watching Seanna across the room, as she stood at her mother's side, Orman noted that they were statuesque women individually but together looked even more empowered—a mother wolf with her pup beside her, watching and learning the skills of the hunt. He had grown accustomed to Seanna's solitary bearing, but the collective strength of her tribe was evident.

"Well, of course, women can fight, but there lies a basic danger in allowing them access to power," Warin noted. "I am sure that such an abomination does not occur in your region."

Orman listened with keen interest, smiling inwardly, knowing that he had found the dissent he sought. *Now, how far can I fan this flame of opposition?*

15

BLOODLINE

At the evening meal, Seanna sat watching Lord Arden and Dian from across the table as they conversed with the men seated around them. Arden had listened attentively throughout the evening, stroking his beard and speaking with measured words when asked questions, while Dian chatted gaily with the lords closest to her.

How fascinating it is to observe my mother in this setting. She is skilled at trivial conversation, yet all the while I know she is also making observations about these men's character.

Seanna also did not miss the discreet glances between her mother and Lord Arden while they sipped their wine. *He watches her, too. He may control his expression, but still, he cannot take his eyes from her face. I am an unwilling voyeur of their secret.*

Seanna remembered how her pulse had quickened upon the Womara's arrival to the township, and even more so when she had walked through the great hall's doors, passing the lines of gathered men to stand before Arden, knowing that he was her father.

The very air in the room had changed as the men stared. Her jaw had tightened under their piercing looks, as they scrutinized the women's every step. Seanna had walked at Dian's side, along with Thea. The remaining women behind them included several members of the Womara council and the younger warriors delegated as Dian's bodyguards. Seanna had held her breath as they stopped before Lord Arden and she measured the weight of her knowledge of their relationship.

I am your blood! she thought silently.

Lord Arden had kept his neutral expression but his gaze remained steadily on Dian as the women had advanced. When they stopped before him, Seanna observed that his eyes seemed to dance with an extra-brilliant light. Seanna had been in Arden's presence many times over the past several years as a member of the alliance scouts, but now all had changed.

I am not sure what he expects of me.

When was the last time her mother and Arden had seen each other? She quickly deduced that it was when Dian had accompanied her to the alliance scout trials. Lord Arden had always been an advocate for the Womara's inclusion in the alliance and had championed Seanna's cause as she became the first female alliance scout.

Did I earn my place? she wondered, but quickly shook off the thought. *I cannot start to question everything that has come to pass. I am confident in my skills and know that I rightly earned my standing among my fellow scouts.*

Her acceptance was a hard-earned triumph for the Womara. That night, exhausted from the trials, Seanna had retired before the celebrations were over and had not questioned her mother's absence from their quarters before she fell asleep.

She must have gone to him that night, and why should she not have? Although I may be reluctant to accept that she is still a woman with needs, or that she has loved this man for as long as she tells me she has, I am the child of that love.

Seanna shifted her attention back to the present as she watched her mother, led by Lord Arden, make additional rounds of formal introductions.

She radiates a certain magnetism and is comfortable with its effects. I imagine that Lord Arden might not be the only man to feel it.

Arden caught her eye for a brief moment and tilted his head to acknowledge her. Seanna stiffened and realized that she had been clenching her sword hilt tightly. She bowed her head, relaxing her grip and placing a hand over her heart. She forced a neutral expression, conscious of her effort not to convey any nuances or gestures beyond the protocols of the moment.

I must concentrate on what is at hand here. I will come to terms with my uncertainty in my own time!

Seanna turned her attention to the men in the room and noted the familiar faces of the alliance council. Her jaw tightened again when she viewed Lord Orman and Lord Warin standing together, awaiting their introduction to her mother. *A pair of foxes from the same lair!*

Her mother circled the room with Lord Arden at her side, stopping before Stuart and Lord Orman first, and then Lord Warin. Lord Warin stood unmoved at first, with a familiar dour expression, but then began to shift restlessly under Dian's scrutiny. Orman returned her direct gaze, effusing charm and speaking accolades, but Seanna noticed his smile quickly fade after she passed.

It will be interesting to hear how my mother judges them.

Throughout the rest of the evening, Seanna watched Orman

mingle among the men with calculated detachment, never staying too long with any one person. As he circulated, his expression shifted from engaging to disinterested once he turned away. She speculated that as an envoy, he projected a reserved decorum in order to maintain distance from the overzealous councilmen pressing him for details. Her candid thoughts were not so generous: *There is no real passion in this man.*

Seanna noted that Orman and Warin seemed particularly engrossed in a private conversation for most of the evening, and she watched Dian's eye linger on the men more than once. Her chest tightened when she saw Lord Arden making his way across the room toward her.

"You have returned to us," he said, smiling at her. "And you have been successful in your journey to reunite the prince with his father."

"Yes, my lord."

"You have also returned with an envoy from this new region who bears proposals for trade from the prince who is now a king. This good fortune could change the lives of many people. It is a great achievement that you have accomplished."

"Thank you again, my lord."

Arden paused for a moment, searching her face, and seemed at a loss for words.

Does he want something more from me? Perhaps a gesture of recognition that I am his daughter?

"I would like to hear more about your journey," Arden said.

"I am at your service, my lord," Seanna replied.

"I will find a time when you and your mother can meet me for a private audience," he said.

Seanna could only nod, as she felt herself flush at the prospect of meeting him alone, and of having to reckon with emotions that she was unwilling to declare. She was relieved when the evening began to wane; the alliance council meeting would begin the next day, and she wanted to be alone.

Dian and Arden spoke briefly, and Seanna caught the quick movement of her mother's hand reaching out to touch his lightly. This gesture of affection was the only physical contact she had seen between them all evening. She then glanced over at Stuart and Thea, who had not left each other's side. She had smiled to herself earlier when Lord Stuart had drawn Thea to him, unable to conceal his delight at being reunited.

They are blessed to be so open in their love for each other. James is so far away. I wish he were here beside me, too.

Seanna and her mother walked toward their quarters, but Dian turned and announced a digression: "Lord Arden has requested a private meeting in his chambers to discuss certain events before the council meets tomorrow."

When Seanna could not help but frown, Dian stopped and asked, "You do not want to meet?"

Seanna hesitated. "I do not feel ready."

Her mother's expression conveyed annoyance. "Seanna, I do not know if there will ever be an ideal time. I conveyed to your father that I have shared his letter. I think he is concerned about what you might be feeling."

"And what do *you* think, Mother? Are you not concerned that I must face this reality in addition to all else that has occurred in the past few months?"

Dian eyed her. "I am, because I know you, Daughter, and although you have trained yourself as a warrior to contain your emotions, I can feel that you struggle with this knowledge."

Seanna lowered her head, knowing the truth of her mother's words.

"Let us talk with him away from all the prying eyes, where every gesture we make is calculated," Dian continued. "You have not had an opportunity to speak with Arden since you stood before the alliance council in anger and then departed for the reunion with your James."

"He does not know your mind either, Mother," Seanna said.

Dian stopped abruptly. "Yes, it is true that he and I need to exchange our own words, but you must also accept that nothing can change the truth of who your father is. It is time to face this fact and let us share everything with you together."

Seanna took a deep breath, feeling herself surrender to the understanding that her mother was right again. *I do acknowledge that many things are changing around me as I struggle to gain control of myself. Why do I fight it?*

Seanna straightened her posture and nodded to her mother that they should go. *I cannot let my uncertainty hamper what needs to happen next.*

The servant leading them knocked softly on the entrance to Lord Arden's chamber, and the door opened into the receiving room of his private quarters.

"Welcome," Arden said, and stepped aside, allowing Dian and Seanna to enter.

He dismissed the servant, and closed the door behind them. Seanna's eyes went wide as her mother did not hesitate, moving to Arden and placing her arms around his neck. She pressed her body close to his and kissed him.

As Seanna watched him gather Dian to him, holding her tight and kissing her in return, she felt color rise into her cheeks and was unsure of where to look.

Arden released his hold and stepped back, looking deeply into Dian's eyes as she searched his face. "How is it with you, my love?" she asked.

"I am still your love?" Arden asked. "I thought the recent events might have changed your heart."

"No, they have not. My whole heart is still yours," Dian replied. "Nothing will ever divide us; the affairs of men cannot change what we have shared."

Arden turned to Seanna, composing himself and giving her a half smile. "We must remember ourselves. I know now that your mother has shared my letter and the secret of your birth."

Seanna nodded but did not speak.

"I think I can guess by your expression that this revelation must have been very astounding and uncomfortable," Arden offered.

Dian stepped toward Seanna, placed a reassuring arm around her shoulder, and turned to Arden. "I did share your words with her before she departed over the mountain. I did not want her to leave without knowing the sentiments of your letter."

Arden drew closer to Seanna as well. "I am glad that your mother has told you, but I can imagine your confusion."

Seanna swallowed hard. "You must give me some time. I was in a state of shock when I left to the mountain peaks, and I still harbored anger over the alliance vote." Her voice quivered a little as she added, "I left overwhelmed and unwilling to consider your words."

"Fair enough." Arden smiled softly at her. "When Dian read my letter to you, my words declared my mindset at the time, including how I questioned her motives behind a concealed negotiation to build a port with Lord Edmond."

"That was not my intent," Dian protested. "An alliance with Lord Edmond to build a port was necessary if we were to be excluded from the council alliance. Seanna sought out Stuart's advice amid her conflict about breaking her oath of secrecy with the prince and revealing their rendezvous. It was then that Stuart revealed to her that his father and I had spoken privately about building the port without the alliance, if necessary. I did not anticipate that she would use Stuart's information to impact the council's decision to place the Womara on the council before she departed to meet the prince."

Arden added, "And she implied that without alliance support as she journeyed into this new region, we would be excluded from the possible establishment of any trading routes and that the Womara would build the port with Lord Edmond."

Dian glanced at Seanna. "It was my error in judgment not to share all truths with her; had I done so, it might have tempered such a threat to the council."

Arden nodded. "Perhaps, but she countermanded my authority and left me questioning your mindset."

"I knew you would question my loyalty," Dian said.

Arden added, "What is done cannot be undone. What is important now is that we are united in the pursuit of our final objective: to build the port. Seanna may have secured the beginning of a future that would have been challenging to achieve without her crossing the mountain again and reuniting with the prince."

Seanna bowed her head to him.

"The discussions tomorrow should be preliminary," Arden declared. "In my opinion, Seanna has met the council's demands.

Signing an agreement with this new king can begin the implementation of the port and the vote for the Womara's inclusion in the council. Let us celebrate that accomplishment."

Arden stepped away to fill three wineglasses, then returned and handed one to both Seanna and Dian. "No more talk of the alliance tonight. I wish to speak with you, Seanna. You must have many questions."

"I must confess that I cannot think with clarity," she answered. *How strange to suddenly feel as if I know so little about either one of these people who stand before me.*

"I understand." Arden smiled. "Come, let's sit before the fire and talk." He settled into his chair and beckoned Dian to seat herself next to him. "Where do we start?" he asked, as Seanna sat on the floor before the fire.

"At the beginning, I would imagine," Seanna said. Arden's expression saddened for a moment, and she realized, *He must be remembering the painful memory of the tragedy that brought him and my mother together.*

Arden stroked his beard as he responded, "I will never forget the day when Dian and her Womara warriors rode into our township, bearing the bodies of my older brother and his men. Her own brother was among the dead, and the Womara carried the bloody heads of the barbarian raiders who had killed them."

Dian reached out and took his hand as he continued. "In my shock and grief, I was ashamed to admit that your mother captivated me from the moment I saw her. She was fierce and splattered in the blood of the dead. Her eyes were wild as she sat high and proud upon her horse, before she cast a raider's head onto the ground before me. I had never seen such a beautiful woman and have yet to know her equal."

Dian squeezed his hand, giving him a warm smile.

"Your mother remained in our township for many months, and before she returned home, we declared and consummated our love, even though we knew we lived in very different worlds. She returned to her forests to bear our child and lead her people."

"It tore my heart in two to leave your father," Dian said.

Arden continued, "Many months before the death of my brother, my father had announced that he had arranged a suitable marriage for me, to a local clan leader's daughter. After your mother departed, I was reluctant not to honor my father's wishes and marry the woman he had chosen. Your mother and I agreed that we would keep your birth a secret."

Arden rose to pour more wine as he went on. "My new bride tried to be a good wife. But she bore me no child, and I could not make her suffer more by revealing the truth of your birth. She died several years later, declaring that she had failed me, and I let her go to her grave wondering why I never really loved her. I could not tell her the hidden truth that I never stopped loving Dian."

Arden's eyes shone in the firelight as he looked at her mother, causing Seanna's heart to ache as she pondered her parents' years of sacrifice.

"As the leaders of our people, we could meet over the years and reinforce our alliances for the protection of the northern regions of our realm," Dian said. "Your father did see you mature but could never embrace you."

"I do recall seeing you when I was a child," Seanna spoke, as Arden smiled at her. "Whose initiative was it that I attend the alliance warrior trials?" she asked.

"It was mine," Arden answered. "I knew it would be an important moment of recognition for the Womara but also, and more important, a first step toward acceptance by and exposure to the world of clansmen through your service in the alliance scouts."

"Do not doubt that you earned your place among those elite scouts," Dian said.

Arden nodded, "Yes, I did have a special interest in your success, but I also knew of your prowess as a warrior through your mother's letters."

"I struggled for many years as it became harder and harder not to tell Seanna all that she is," Dian added.

"Who else knew?" Seanna asked.

'Only your grandmother Landra," Dian said. "I was to be chosen the new leader of the Womara, and she sent me to bring my brother, Dane, home for the celebration. After his death, I remained in Arden's township, and when I returned to the forest, I knew I carried his child. I told only her, and she directed me to dance at the fire rites at the full moon. I selected a man that night so no one would question the timing of your birth."

Seanna nodded, sitting upright. "You rarely speak of your brother, and I do not remember him."

"You were only a small child, and the memory is still too painful to recount," Dian said, turning away. "But tonight, I will share everything."

16

TWIN LIVES

Dian walked arm in arm with her mother, Landra, along the trails leading through the forest and into the market square of the Womara township.

"What is it that you want to talk to me about, Mother?" Dian asked.

Landra turned to her and reached out to hold her daughter's shoulders. "I wish to tell you that I have made a decision and am about to declare my choice for our next leader."

Dian's eyes went wide at Landra's next words: "It will be you."

Dian stammered, "I am honored, Mother, but you have many more years to be our leader."

Landra nodded. "Possibly, but I have decided that it is time. I have already spoken to our council. As you know, the succession of a Womara leader does not always pass from mother to daughter, but they are very pleased with my choice."

Dian bowed her head and placed her hand upon her heart. "Then I am honored."

"You have some trials before you take the role of leader," Landra said, giving her a half smile, "though nothing too challenging—only a gesture of service outside the familiarity of this forest."

Dian raised an eyebrow. "What do you suggest I do?"

"Your brother has been gone for several years now in service to Lord Alfred, my old friend and ally who stood beside the Womara in the great invasion. He stayed among us while we buried our dead, and afterward I journeyed to his township, where he championed and wrote the treaty that granted us our land. Our alliance has been strong all these years."

"My brother speaks highly of him," Dian said.

"I lived among them for several months and gained useful insights into the ways of men. His sons, Richard and Arden, will be valuable allies to our people in the future. Richard is the eldest son and the clan successor of his father's region."

Dian listened intently to her mother's words, questioning their direction. "These are new times calling for younger leaders," Landra said, as she stared into her daughter's eyes. "I have some time to prepare you for that leadership." Then she cast her gaze downward. "I did not have this opportunity. When my mother died in battle, there was no other to lead. I was too young for such responsibility, but what choice did I have?" Dian watched as her mother's eyes filled with tears.

"I learned much by living among men for a time, and at my directive, it is now a Womara decree that a prospective new leader should venture out in service to a lord. It served me well the time I stayed within Lord Alfred's township."

"You did not have to live among them for long, Mother," Dian noted. "You brought my father here, did you not?"

Landra smiled. "Yes, and it was the wisest decision I have ever made. Look around at all the trade merchants that comprise this marketplace."

Dian smiled, admiring the commerce of the town's center.

"Have I told you that your father was the first man to bring trade to the Womara?"

"Many times," Dian said, laughing.

Landra looked away wistfully. "I miss him every day."

Dian squeezed her mother's arm. "So do I."

Landra gave her a reassuring smile. "He was a special man and brought great joy into my life. But no joy between the two of us could equal that which we experienced on the day of your and your brother's birth."

Dian grimaced and could not meet her mother's eyes.

"I see in your face that you are missing your brother," Landra said.

"How can I not? We were born within minutes of each other, and we have not known many moments without each other's company," Dian confessed. "I know he left the Womara at the appointed age to serve among men, but I am sure that he will return one day to live with us again."

Landra nodded. "We shall see. That is his choice. In the meantime, you must prepare to be a clan leader."

"My brother has pledged his service to Lord Alfred. Does that not further our goodwill enough?" Dian asked.

"Dane's experiences are not the same, and you know that, even though you are so similar and often claim to have the same thoughts," her mother said.

Dian nodded, keeping her thoughts to herself. *Yes, but I dislike the prospect of living among the townships of men.*

"In truth, Daughter, I am tired and my heart aches as I lose those dear to me. After Asha's death, three years ago, and your father's, not even a full changing of the seasons, you and your brother are the last of my joys." She smiled, reaching out to touch Dian's cheek. "It has been a long fight. I wish to step aside if you are ready."

Dian looked at her mother's face. She had aged in the past year. Her bronzed hair was now almost completely covered in gray, her eyes duller and losing their luster.

Dian stood proudly. "I am ready to serve and to honor your wishes."

"Good." Landra squeezed her shoulders. "I want you to ride out and meet your brother, who is escorting Lord Richard here as my guest. It will be a celebration of our future and the strength of our new, young leaders."

Dian smiled, her heart beating quickly at hearing her mother refer to her as a leader. *Am I ready?*

Landra's words interrupted her thoughts. "I assumed they would have arrived by now, but I am sure they have just lingered in a village. Take a dozen Womara scouts with you to accompany them back," she ordered. "We will talk more when you return."

Dian and the Womara scouts traveled the known route toward the outlying boundaries of Lord Alfred's region, where Dian thought she would meet up with Lord Richard and his men. The scouts who had ridden ahead returned at full gallop, having found the tracks of many horses diverting from the main pathways only hours earlier.

Dian's skin tingled, and the hairs on her arm stood on end. *So many men. Who could they be?*

The scouts followed tracks that turned away into a small canyon, and the women descended upon a slaughter. A dozen men lay strewn about the ground, murdered to the last one. They appeared to have been surprised and pinned against the rock gorge before they could escape. Some were killed brutally, and all were stripped of their possessions and weapons. Half of the horses were gone; the remaining animals milled together in a small grove of trees.

Dian's heart beat wildly as she searched the faces of the dead men, before spying the prone body of her brother. She leaped from her horse to his side, yelling, "No! No!"

Dane was lying on his back, eyes wide open and a fatal wound in the center of his chest. Dian sobbed as she touched his body, before rearing her head back in a primal scream.

A Womara scout held back another woman who wanted to rush to her side. "Leave her alone for a moment," she cautioned.

Dian sat cradling her dead brother's body and rocking him back and forth in her arms as if she could breathe life back into his inert form. Little by little, she stopped moving and gently placed him on the ground, before slowly rising and ordering two women to her side. The other scouts moved among the remaining men, checking the bodies.

Dian still could not take her eyes from her brother, but she asked, "And Lord Richard?"

"He is here, and he was mutilated," the scout reported.

Dian walked to the fallen lord and gazed down at the corpse. Seeing that he had been stabbed repeatedly and his throat cut made her blood boil.

"These killings look like the acts of north raiders," a scout announced, "and their tracks are heading to the coast."

"These men are animals," Dian said, "and so we will hunt them as such."

"Stay here and guard the bodies and the horses," she told two Womara scouts. "The murderers are only a couple of hours ahead of us. We will run them down!"

The Womara women rode hard to catch the raiders at the edge of the vast forest. A ride across the open plain and the men would reach the coastline, where, Dian suspected, a waiting boat would be their means of escape.

When the men came into view, the women spurred their horses, and their cries, combined with the sounds of the galloping animals, startled the raiders into turning and facing their pursuers. Knowing that the Womara were about to overtake them, the men jumped from their horses and stood in tight formation, weapons in hand.

The lead Womara riders shot arrows into some of the front men, felling them as the rest of the mounted women cut the raiders with swords or trampled them.

"They are women!" one man yelled, before a warrior slashed his throat with her descending sword.

Dian yelled out, "Don't kill them all! I want their leader," as the Womara archers surrounded the remaining, outnumbered men, keeping them pinned together in a tight cluster.

Dian dismounted from her horse, walking among them. Half a dozen lay dead, and the other half were being bound and forced to their knees by women with bows drawn and arrows pointed at the men's chests. "Who is your leader?" Dian demanded.

One man rose, struggling, to his feet. "I am," he boasted.

"Tie him to that tree," Dian ordered. The women forced him against a large sapling and bound him to it by his throat, pinning him to the trunk.

"You expect me to beg for my life?" the leader mocked. "We are Northmen and will die like men, not cowering at the hands of a bunch of women."

"We shall see about that," Dian retorted. "For you have crossed the paths of the Womara clan today, killing one of our own, and you will die like the dogs that you are."

"You mean like the men we killed," he taunted.

"My brother was among those men," Dian said, her voice growing stronger.

"Then he must have been the one who begged on his knees for his life," the leader said, laughing.

"You lie!" she yelled, as she struck him across the face with the blunt edge of her sword. "He was a Womara and a warrior."

Her eyes narrowed as she stepped closer, and with the blade of her sword she carved a line slowly across his chest, causing him to grunt in pain as blood trickled down his chest.

Still, the raider managed another sneer. "You will not keep me from walking with honor to the halls of my waiting ancestors. I will stand proudly before them today."

"No," Diane said, leering, "you will crawl across the door of your ancestors' hall in pieces." She lifted his chin with her sword, forcing him to look into her eyes. "And I will take the heads of you and all your men on spikes to the township of the ones you have killed."

The raiders on their knees struggled against their binds, only for the Womara to grab their hair and hold swords at their throats.

"Watch your men die first," Dian said, nodding to the women, who gripped each man's hair tightly and slashed his throat.

Dian watched the leader's expression darken as he listened to the guttural gasps of his dying men. As the Womara warriors let their victims' bodies fall forward in the dirt, she taunted, "No glory in that death, on their knees, no sword in hand, and killed by women, no less. I am sure your ancestors will spend the rest of eternity mocking you."

The raider eyed her with loathing as she paced before him. "You are all witches," he hissed.

Dian threw down her sword, drew her knife, and stepped to him, driving the blade into his chest and watched his eyes gape before she twisted it into his heart. When his head dropped forward in death, she cut the bind on his throat and watched dispassionately as he fell to the ground with a loud thud. After she had steadied her breathing, she ordered, "Cut off their heads."

When the Womara departed, Dian glanced back at the grisly scene. The headless bodies of the raiders lay scattered on the ground, red with their blood. The leader lay on his back with a "W" carved into his bare chest and a single Womara arrow driven through his heart.

At sunset, the women rode through the gates of Lord Alfred's township and the people stopped to stare speechlessly as they thundered by on horseback toward the center of town, carrying spikes with the heads of the raiders and the bodies of the men's victims.

Wails rang out as the townspeople recognized their loved ones' corpses strapped to the horses, and the crowd followed as the women rode to the doors of the lord's hall. Lord Alfred and his son Arden emerged to the clamor of the people. Upon seeing the body of his son, Alfred cried out and rushed to him.

"Take him down," he ordered. As the men gently laid his son before him, he looked up at Dian, his face stricken. "What happened here?" he demanded.

Dian dismounted and stood before him, bowing her head. "Lord Alfred, I am Dian, the daughter of Landra of the Womara. At my mother's bidding, we were traveling to meet Lord Richard's party and happened upon this slaughter. We hunted down the raiders before they escaped and came to return your dead and the heads of those who took their lives."

The elder lord stumbled and reached out, seeking the arm of his son as he tried to stand. Arden rushed to his side, lifting him to his feet and away from the sight of his dead son.

Arden spoke to her gently: "Dian, does your brother not lie here among the dead?"

Her shoulders sagged, her grief renewed. "Yes, and I will take my leave to take him home to our forest and my mother," she answered.

Lord Alfred, still holding his son's arm, stepped toward her and said, "You have done us a great service in avenging the death of my son and his men. What can I give you in exchange?"

Dian stood tall. "I ask nothing of you, my lord, save for the body of my brother."

Lord Alfred reached to touch her forearm. "Stay with us. We will build the funeral pyres together, as I once did with your mother, and we will honor the deaths of these men. Let us share our grief."

Dian hesitated, glancing back at Dane's body, her lip trembling, then turned and searched Alfred and Arden's faces.

"My brother would have wanted that honor, and I thank you. We will stay to build his fire and then return his ashes to his home."

Dian looked into the eyes of the young Lord Arden, who had not taken his eyes from her, and she could not stop her thoughts. *What a striking man.* He was tall, with broad shoulders and inky hair that fell to his shoulders. His light stubble of beard did not cover his well-defined jawline, and his dark brows set off deep-set, ice-blue eyes that brightened his face, even in grief.

Dian and the Womara scouts remained for the funeral rites over the next three days. She had received word from her mother to send back Dane's ashes to her, along with a request that Dian take her brother's place in service to Lord Alfred.

Lord Alfred gladly accepted her offer, and she knelt before the lord, her hand over her heart, as she honored her mother's command. Her eyes met Arden's as he stood by his father, and he smiled. *I cannot look away*, she thought.

Over the next several moons, the great lord declined in health, his spirit broken and his will to live lost, and passed the mantle of leadership to his remaining son. As Dian stood observing the ceremony that decreed Arden the next clan leader, she reflected, *We will be the leaders of our people. I now understand the wisdom of my mother's directive, for we are our clans' future.*

Her heart warmed with that new awareness, and she embraced the path she had been placed upon. A piece of her heart had died along with her brother, but it now fluttered once more, renewed with the stirrings of love as she watched Arden standing before his people.

17

THE FOX'S LAIR

Lord Orman made his way through the township's dark alleyways as he searched for the tavern where Lord Warin had arranged to meet him. He stepped lightly over the rutted, narrow dirt streets that worsened as he walked deeper into the more unsavory section of town. He covered his face against unpleasant smells that conjured unwelcome memories of the clandestine days of his youth, living among the filth who existed on the edges of human decency. *What in hell's name am I doing down here?*

After the evening's festivities with Lord Arden and the councilmen had ended, Lord Warin had approached Orman, declaring urgently that they needed to talk, and asked him to a private meeting. Orman had observed that Warin's request to meet coincided with the arrival of a young man in the meeting hall who had sought Warin out and spent time speaking privately with him.

Is whatever the young man brought to Warin's attention the reason for his request? Orman wondered now. *And why Warin's*

*choice of such a remote location for our meeting? It signals to me
that he does not wish the prying eyes of the council to see us.*

At the next turn, he viewed the sign with a carved wild boar
that hung above the door. Slipping into the dark interior, he
recoiled at the smell of stale ale, men's sweat, and a faint trace
of urine. When he spotted Warin beckoning from a dark corner,
Orman made his way past the blank stares of the rough-looking
patrons and seated himself across from the lord and the same
young man Orman had seen conversing with Warin earlier.

Warin slammed the tankard of ale he was drinking on the
table with a loud clank. "I told you he would come," he boasted,
turning to the younger man. "Lord Orman, let me introduce you
to my nephew, Dunstan."

Dunstan tilted his head in greeting, and Orman acknowledged him briefly, before turning back to Warin, saying, "I hope
that you have a good reason to request my presence at this hour
and in such a place," as he glanced around the room again.

"This place serves my purpose, for Lord Arden's halls have
ears," Warin retorted.

Orman looked around the room. "And what purpose is that?"
he answered with a curled lip. "This meeting could be viewed as
compromising my position with the council, so let us get on with
it. What do you need to discuss?"

Warin's eyes narrowed. "Compromising, yes, but you still
came," he declared. "Nevertheless, I will get to the point." He
looked sideways at his nephew and explained, "At my orders,
Dunstan has remained in the township of Lord Edmond, posing
as a merchant for the past several months. I sent him there after
the departure of the Womara woman to the mountains, and he
remained until she returned recently by sea."

"Why, Lord Warin? How did you know that she would return at all?" Orman asked.

"I did not," Warin answered. "I sought to gather information. A port built in Edmond's township was proposed by the council and I wished to monitor that no construction was implemented."

"I thought the council's decree was very specific. They would allow time to await a possible outcome if and when Seanna returned from the region—was that not the decree?" Orman asked.

Warin nodded. "True, they waited. But I did not trust the female clan. I wanted to make sure that they did not think of proceeding against the council's decrees and begin building a port."

Orman leaned back in his chair, tapping the table with his fingers.

"I understood that they were free to act outside those council decrees if they chose to. These points all seem moot at this juncture, do they not? For it appears that things are changing for the better, as my presence as an envoy bringing agreements bears out."

"The better for whom?" Waring retorted. "Let me be more precise in my concerns. I have always been candid about my desire for a second port location, in my region, to be considered, but the council has never seriously considered my suggestion."

"What can I do about that, Lord Warin, when your council seems set on a different course?"

"I want you to change their minds." Warin leaned back with a half-smile on his face.

"And why would I do that?" Orman tapped a single finger on the table.

"For the opportunity to be the port master overseeing all trade between the new regions. I have heard that he who holds that position will be made wealthy beyond his dreams."

Orman laughed. "I am envoy to the king and a wealthy man in my own right."

"But an envoy who might fail in his mission may not wish to return to his city in disgrace." Warin leered as he glanced at Dunstan.

"And why would I fail?" Orman asked, narrowing his eyes.

Warin signaled to his nephew, who leaned in closer to speak. "I waited weeks in the township of Lord Edmond to learn from my spies that the lord had received a message informing him that Seanna would return soon by sea to his port."

Where is this going? I already know this, Orman thought.

Dunstan continued, "This was not the information that I wanted to report to my uncle, but I waited for her arrival and watched among the crowd that had gathered as she disembarked to the tributes of those onshore. She was accompanied by you, my lord, with your entourage of mappers and surveyors to plot a trade route and, I assumed, to start building the port."

Warin crossed his arms across his chest and shook his head. "I was disappointed to hear that Seanna returned from the north triumphant."

"Why?" Orman asked.

"I thought she lied about the pass through the mountains," Warin answered. "Or that the prince she traveled to meet did not exist. Or that if he did, he had forgotten their oath and she would not return to stand before the council again."

Orman eyed him, thinking, *I have heard of Warin's rancor against the women's clan from the other councilmen, but the words from his own lips reveal the depth of his vindictiveness.*

He recalled the councilmen's conversations about Seanna's open defiance of council after the vote and her decision to travel alone into this unknown territory. But her refusal to reveal the location of the pass to the council was what had truly inflamed Warin.

"Well, she has triumphed," Orman goaded.

"Yes, it appears so on the surface," Warin said, as Orman felt the smug smile fade from his face.

Dunstan added, "The ship arriving from your city has crews with tongues that can be loosened with drink and coin."

"And what information did you buy?" Orman asked.

"I learned that it is common knowledge that Seanna did rescue and gain the favor of a prince left for dead in an assassination attempt that killed his father. He was crowned king because she found him and returned him to his people."

"Yes, yes." Orman shifted in his chair impatiently. "What does any of this have to do with the port?"

"I have information that could be a possible impediment to the building of any port," Warin said.

Orman's chest constricted at the prospect of an unwelcome disclosure.

Dunstan continued, "My spies also reported that the man who assassinated the king is alive and safe. The guilt rests on the king's cousin Thomas, who had fled the kingdom and now lives in exile and under the protection of the barbarian King Havlor of the North. There are rumors that this cousin seeks your king's throne and that conflict could be looming."

Orman winced, cursing under his breath. *I had hoped to stay ahead of such a disclosure.*

"It is rumored that this young king builds a new military council around him. Does he prepare for the possibility of war?" Warin asked.

Orman sat silently, staring at the two men, until Warin posed another question: "How do you think the council will perceive any negotiations knowing that you did not fully disclose your king's vulnerability? I assume his envoy is aware of these developments?"

Orman narrowed his eyes at the implied threat. "Men prepare for war all the time. Our king is wise to be vigilant."

"But are we not at risk, too, in this association with the new king?" Warin asked, leaning forward. "And the Womara woman? She brings an empty victory if we align with a new region at war. How could the council trust her for not revealing all the truths she holds?"

Orman frowned. "Do you imply that the alliance will forgo the opportunity for an agreement? Or is your distate for the women's clan clouding your reason?"

"No, my reasoning is clear," Warin answered, lifting his tankard of ale and drinking it down. He shrugged. "You cannot deny that this development could be perceived as a risky alliance if a conflict is growing," he added, as he wiped his beard with the back of his hand.

Orman felt his forehead furrow into an involuntary frown as Warin spoke again: "Or this preparation for war could be viewed as a great opportunity." He smiled at Dunstan, then slapped his hand on the table before him, signaling for more ale. "I thought that I was thwarted in my quest for a port in my region when Seanna's reunion with the king was successful."

How long do we have to play this chess game? Orman wondered.

"But maybe the alliance is too hasty in praising her," Warin cautioned. "Or remiss in not questioning her about how she obtained the terms with which she has returned."

"Why would the council question the terms? And I hope you did not bring me here to reveal details that I am not at liberty to discuss," Orman said.

Warin smiled smugly. "No, but I would speculate that any terms will favor the women's clan, for she has earned more than just the king's favor."

"What do you mean?" Orman asked.

Dunstan spoke up: "Rumor has it that she shares not only a vision of a new alliance with your king, and the obvious mutual benefits to both regions, but also his bed."

Orman's chest constricted again. *Warin's nephew certainly has the talent to root out information. I had hoped to use such a volatile disclosure at an appropriate time, if needed, and certainly not in the hands of a manipulator like Warin.*

"I was shocked to hear of such a union," Warin said. "What kind of a king would be attracted to such a woman?"

"There was a bond that formed when she rescued him, and there is truth to the fact that she possesses more than just the king's gratitude for his life," Orman confessed. "But it does not change the agreements at hand."

Does he judge how far he can press me? Orman thought.

"Well, who knows what she offered him? She is a woman, after all, and what woman wouldn't whore herself to gain such a conquest?" Warin retorted.

"Be cautious in your loose words," Orman warned, shifting in his chair. "I do not believe that the Womara wish to act outside the alliance. But if you incite divisiveness with your accusations, they could move to build the port without the alliance's support."

"And I suspect that your king will condone that," Warin huffed.

"I cannot understand the minds of men who would live under the thumb of an alliance that will allow the dictates of the female clan—"

Dunstan interjected, "Uncle, Lord Orman is right. You could undermine your objective with this malevolence."

Orman watched Warin's face. *Wise words to heed. Your nephew may possess a special talent for gathering information, but he is even more valuable if he can rein you in!*

Warin nodded to his nephew as his lips curled into a half smile. "I can cooperate if you give support to my claim for the consideration of another port, Lord Orman. I ask only for the council's ear, so that I may consider a second option in light of this new information and cast the shadow of a doubt with the suggestion of impending warfare."

Is this something I want to do? Orman asked himself.

Warin continued, "Keep this in mind: Your king would need both a port in a larger region and the men to build it if war were to come. We can provide that," he declared proudly.

"Is there something more, Lord Warin?" Orman asked.

"And if the port is built in my region, the women's clan will have no part of it."

Orman leaned back, stroking his beard, before he rose from his chair. "I have heard enough," he announced. "I will not disclose the king's position, but I can be reticent to announce any proclamation of the port construction at this gathering."

Warin's smile faded as Orman cautioned, "Do not take liberties because we have spoken in private or because you feel as if we are now familiar, for we are not. I will deny any talks if you disclose them. But if you were to bring your allegations before the council, they may be enough to delay the signing of any agreements, especially if I propose to travel to your region to judge its location for its suitability as a port."

Warin grinned broadly and offered his hand to shake, but Orman ignored it. "One last warning, Lord Warin: You must appear conciliatory in offering your information for consideration by the alliance, as well as inclusive of the women's clan. For my part, I will only be acting within my duty to consider all viable options," he concluded.

Warin lowered his hand but nodded his understanding.

As Orman turned to hasten away from his company, he had one bright thought: *I may have found the opportunity to provide Thomas with the weak link that I have sought, and an opening to the southern coastline made vulnerable to attack by this ambitious and self-serving clan lord.*

18

THE TRAP IS LAID

It was late in the evening when Seanna rose to leave Lord Arden's chambers. She stretched her body and rolled her stiff shoulders, as she viewed her parents sitting next to each other, still holding hands. When Dian had finished the account of her first meeting with Arden and their blossoming love, Seanna had searched for words to articulate what she was feeling, but had been able to describe only the comfort she derived from knowing her parents' story and surrendering to understanding a piece of herself more deeply.

The tension in her chest had lessened through the telling of her mother's tale, replaced with a growing warmth in her heart as she looked at her mother in a new light. She saw Dian as a person just like any other woman: She loved, had endured tragedy, and had exacted vengeance with detached cruelty while at the same time fighting fiercely to protect her people.

Dian rose to walk her to the door, and Seanna reached out to grasp her hand. "I want you to share everything with my father."

Arden glanced up from his seat when she called him "father," his eyes glistening, and smiled warmly.

"Tell him about James and me," Seanna said.

Dian nodded, reaching out to embrace her as Arden walked over to stand close to her mother, placing his arm around her waist.

"I am at peace with all you have shared tonight." Seanna smiled shyly, bidding them farewell as she closed the door behind her. Her body tingled as she walked into the chill night air, and she rubbed her hands to retain the warmth of the fire she had just left. *My spirit feels lighter, and my love for James has grown even deeper* .

She walked across the silent compound, entering her quarters, dropping her clothes quickly, and slipping into bed. She curled her body tightly within the blankets, wrapping her arms around herself to ward off the chill.

Hearing what her parents had forgone to raise her in secrecy and conceal their relationship had changed all her prior perceptions of them and softened her judgments. In that moment of illumination, she felt a greater intimacy with both of them. Their years of silently holding their love close to their hearts revealed their deeper sense of duty; as leaders of their clans, they had ultimately forfeited their own needs for the good of their people.

Then a dark thought crossed her mind: *Have I seen a window into my future and a similar fate for James and me—pledged in love but living apart for years to serve our people?*

Seanna hugged her body more tightly, thinking, *I long to talk with him; my heart is lighter at the thought of seeing him soon,* before she fell into a deep slumber.

She slept soundly for several hours but rolled over sometime in the early hours before dawn to view her mother's empty bed. When the first rays of sunlight crept into the darkened room, she smiled as her mother quietly entered their chamber and slipped between the covers.

"We leave for the beginning of the council meeting in a couple of hours," Seanna whispered. "You will suffer for your lack of sleep today," she teased.

"Some things are worth the deprivation," Dian whispered back.

At midmorning, Seanna and Dian entered the meeting hall together. The large room already hummed with the voices of men in conversation. The air felt charged with anticipation, which, Seanna supposed, was fueled by the council's eagerness to begin talks about the alliance.

"This is a good day, Daughter," Dian said.

Seanna nodded while glancing around the room, noting several of the Womara councilwomen mingling among the small groups of men, smiling and at times laughing. Lord Arden was with Orman and several councilmen; the envoy stood with his hands clasped casually in front of his body and nodded to the men with a familiar detachment Seanna now recognized.

I will give him his due. He does look resplendent in a long, flowing, dark robe, and every inch the envoy representing a new region. This will be his defining moment, she thought.

Arden excused himself when he saw them and grinned broadly as he crossed the room to join them.

"Good morning." His eyes lingered on Dian.

"It *is* a good morning," she answered.

Arden looked around the room. "This the first time in

many months that I have witnessed the clansmen in such a positive mood. I hope that this will be a harbinger of many days to come."

Seanna smiled. "I understand their enthusiasm. This is the fulfillment of a personal mission for me and the conclusion of a long journey. I feel the excitement of being part of a new beginning."

Arden said, "Your mother has shared your happiness with me, and I celebrate the news of you and James."

Seanna flushed faintly at his words. When she noticed Stuart and Thea entering the hall, she excused herself to join them. Thea smiled radiantly when she caught Seanna's eye and hastened across the room to meet her. Beaming, she said, "It seems as if it has been a hundred years since we last talked."

"Well, you have been occupied," Seanna teased, as she gestured at Stuart.

"All is well," Thea gushed, "and Stuart cannot contain himself at the prospect of the alliance being on the brink of signing an agreement today."

"I think everyone feels the same," Seanna agreed.

"Stuart has already asked that, after the completion of the port, I voyage with him to be the first of our realm to visit your king's city."

"It is worth the journey," Seanna said. "Perhaps we shall go together. In the meantime, I have something to ask of you."

"Yes, anything."

"After today's gathering and the signing of the trade agreement, the alliance council will have many decisions to make about how to proceed, but I will need to leave."

"Leave where?" Thea asked.

"I will depart for our valley and back to the mountain pass,"

Seanna said. "I hate to take you away from Stuart, but I have need of your service. We will not be gone long."

"But why? Your place is here. You have earned it."

"I cannot speak of anything within this hall, but I need you to come with me. I will tell you everything away from the township."

Seanna watched Thea's forehead furrow while she thought. "You know I trust you in everything, so there must be a good reason behind your request," she answered. "What do I tell Stuart?"

"Tell him you will go as my bodyguard."

Seanna returned to her mother's side, her stomach fluttering as she waited for the gathering to commence. She surveyed the room again as men began to seat themselves at the long tables facing the front dais, where Arden sat with Lord Orman at his side.

Would they begin by reading the agreement that Orman held in his hand? The alliance would have its trading rights granted, based on a coalition of regions and the merchants representing every clan's interest in the township's new port. The king would leave his master architect to assist with the optimal expansion of the port, as well as build some of the infrastructure needed to move trade goods to the connecting townships and clan regions. Seanna knew the contents of the agreement's outline because James had read it to her. *It is a generous offer that all clans of the alliance will share in.*

Though it was not written on the parchment, James had voiced a final decree to Lord Orman that gave her the only pause. James had declared to his envoy that the Womara and Lord Edmond's region would control the issuing of merchant trading rights, and Seanna knew that her mother wanted the port-master rights.

In Arden's chambers the previous night, he had complimented Dian on a brilliant strategy that guaranteed the future of the Womara, building a port either with the alliance or with Lord Edmond. But to be the one who controlled the merchant trade rights was a position that men coveted and would fight for. Dian had openly pressed for the surety of those rights, declaring that Seanna had earned them by saving the king's life, before Arden had tempered her expectation with cautionary words: "There is no need to flaunt any advantage you may feel Seanna is owed. Do not forget that you also seek a place on the alliance council for the Womara and must work with these men."

Dian argued, "I will respect the collective interest of the alliance and do seek cooperation, but we have first rights through the words of the king."

Seanna had cautioned her mother, too, reminding her that no provision within the agreement addressed any debt owed for the life of the king, or that the Womara were owed any rights.

"But did the king not express that directly to the envoy Lord Orman?" Dian asked.

She will fight hard for the privilege that I understand is mine, but I cannot use James's love for me to force that hand.

Seanna had watched her mother's expression as Dian eyed her, gauging her reserve.

All will transpire as it was meant to be. Orman knows the king's directive. But I will feel more settled once all is agreed upon and the first glasses of wine toast to the signing.

Seanna looked around the room again, her eyes resting on Lord Warin, who stood with his arms crossed at his chest, speaking to his nephew at his side. He concluded with a haughty stance of hands on his hips, giving the nephew's shoulder a reassuring slap before seating himself. He surveyed the room, too, and when he noted Seanna, his twisted smile made chills run up her arms.

That is the same look of malice I experienced many months ago when we stood in the very same place. What can he be up to?

Orman had seated himself next to Lord Arden, noting a slightly sick sensation in his stomach as he stared out at the rows of long tables and the expectant faces of the seated clansmen. *The lords all wait with bated breath, but it is uncertain how this day will end.*

Lord Arden called for order, and the conversation subsided when he seated himself. "My lords and ladies, we commence this day by recognizing this most auspicious time for the alliance. It is the dawn of a new beginning and of a future built on progress. Welcome, all."

As cheers rang out, Arden directed his next comments toward Seanna. "Seanna of the Womara clan has returned safely to stand before us, as she pledged, and I will be the first to congratulate her and celebrate her safe return."

Seanna bowed her head to the accolades from Lord Arden and the "ayes" of the crowd as Arden signaled for her to stand and speak.

"My lords," she began, "it seems not long ago that I stood before you last. I have returned humbled by what I have seen in this new and exciting realm and have witnessed an abundance that I hope we will all share. I am gratified to have fulfilled my oath to a king and come back to stand again before you today."

The men's hands rapped the table in unison.

Orman listened closely to Seanna's statement. No rebukes or adversarial words to the council for her previous treatment, only positive sentiments. When she had stood, tall and proud, before

James' advisory council the day before their departure, she had used the same optimistic language, assuming the role of the empowered emissary that she was. Her direct eye gaze and strong words had conveyed confidence as she recounted that she would soon be standing before the alliance. She would be pleased to convey the goodwill of this region's people, the fortitude and generosity of their king, and his willingness to embrace a new endeavor between new realms. She had thanked the king's council for the honor to be a voice alongside their envoy, casting an eye toward Orman. Her words carried potency and had moved the king's councilmen.

At the time, Orman recalled, *I thought that it would be impossible to quell this woman's compelling voice; she almost had me convinced of the possibility of equality and peace between our realms.*

Lord Arden's words interrupted Orman's thoughts: "Seanna has returned with the gratitude of a king and an envoy of his city, ready to discuss a union that is of great benefit to all. The agreements that I have had the privilege of viewing with Lord Orman include all clans of the alliance."

The clansmen gave a round of "ayes" and slapped their fists upon the table again as Orman looked at Lord Warin, who sat unmoving, arms crossed over his chest. His sour expression contrasted sharply with Dian's, whose smile and nods conveyed pride to her daughter.

Yes, Dian is a powerful force, and we shall see whether Warin can pierce the veneer of all this goodwill when the signing of a treaty is diverted and the prospect of trading rights could shift.

Seanna seated herself before Arden spoke again: "Before I ask Lord Orman to begin distilling the terms of the documents on the table before us, there is one matter for the council to consider. We must collectively honor our decree to Seanna and the Womara."

The men nodded in acknowledgment.

"She has returned to stand before us again and accomplished much more, as Lord Orman's presence here supports. There can be no question that the Womara have earned the right to an alliance seat."

The men's hands hitting the table voiced their agreement.

"I move for their immediate inclusion in this council and the alliance," Arden said, scanning the room. "Any opposed, raise your voice now."

Lord Warin stood up slowly from his seat. Orman watched Dian turn with surprise and a scowl upon her face.

"I have a question to pose," Warin announced. "If the Womara fail to be included in the alliance, will the agreements on the table be withdrawn?"

All heads now twisted to view Warin with expressions of shock; some men glared at him. He added quickly, "Do we have such short memories that we are ready to forget the Womara's threat to build a coalition without the alliance?"

"It is forgotten," a man shouted from a back table. "Sit down, Lord Warin."

"I ask only for clarity," Warin said. "I caution against signing any agreement that binds us to a region under threat."

There was a collective intake of breath from the room.

"What does he speak of?" a second man shouted. "Let the envoy answer."

Orman tried to look surprised, leaning forward. "My lords, it is well known among you by now that the cousin who assassinated the king's father fled to the North, where he resides under the sanctuary of King Havlor. Barbarians have always threatened exposed coastlines, including your own, and are known for raiding small, vulnerable villages. Why would King Havlor pose a threat by providing protection to a renegade cousin with no power or arms? The king's cousin offers nothing that the barbarians cannot already take for themselves."

"Is there not more?" Warin asked, as he seated himself.

Orman watched Dian's eyes flash in anger, before she rose to speak directly to Warin: "A trading coalition does not bind men to war. We speculate about issues that have little bearing on the treaty we may hold with this king. The Womara stand here now in cooperation and with a willingness to build unity as an alliance first. We seek only a place at the alliance council's table—one that my daughter has earned. There is nothing more."

The men nodded among themselves, murmuring "aye" as Dian seated herself.

Arden's voice carried disdain when he asked, "Why do you attempt to cast a dark cloud over these talks, Lord Warin?"

Some of the men smirked at the rebuttal as Warin shifted forward in his seat, squaring his shoulders and looking directly at Dian again.

"I did not mean to insult you, Lady Dian, but it is not only the threat of conflict that I speak of. Your daughter possesses an advantage of more than just the goodwill of the king—one that some might deem an unfair point from which to begin negotiations."

Seanna watched the color rise on her mother's face as she felt the blood drain from her own, and she gripped the hilt of her knife under the table to keep her expression composed, suspecting where Warin was going with his words.

He continued, "I wish only to suggest that because of her"—he paused dramatically—"shall we say, 'intimate relationship' with the king, all options may not have been presented in an equal light."

All eyes turned to view her, and she flushed under the scrutiny. *How has this become known to him?* She glanced at Orman, who sat placidly and would not meet her eye. *This is a trap.*

She watched her mother's jaw muscles tighten. "And what alternatives do you refer to?" Dian asked sharply. "Speak, Lord Warin. The council has no time for your game-playing."

"I play no games," Warin retorted. "I seek to ensure that all conditions that could affect the outcome of this council's efforts are presented equitably. We have an envoy here with the expertise to judge these matters with a balanced perspective."

"What balanced perspective?" Lord Arden snapped.

"That any consideration of other ports does not fall subject to favoritism," Warin answered.

"Your region was never the most viable option," Arden retorted, "and you misled Lord Orman if you presented it as such."

"Lord Orman is not under a directive to evaluate other locations," Seanna exclaimed, as she lost her composure.

"And why not?" Warin asked. "Have you already influenced the king's decision?"

Seanna's temper flared at the challenge, before Dian rose with clenched fists and snapped, "How dare you? What is the purpose of such an accusation?"

"Well, let her deny it, then," Warin said. "My nephew has returned from Lord Edmond's township, where it is common knowledge among the ship's crew you traveled with that she keeps close company with the king."

"Do you know of this, Lord Orman?" Warin tested.

Orman rose to face the men, feigning hesitation. "You place me at a great disadvantage, Lord Warin. I am here as the envoy to King James. I do know Lady Seanna to be a woman for whom I believe the king has the deepest respect and affection. And, out of gratitude, he did decree that the Womara carry his special favor."

Seanna sat rigidly, her heart pounding and her blood rushing, as she felt the stares of the men in the room.

Orman pushed on: "My directive is to secure an agreement from the alliance that will produce the greatest mutual success of our two regions. The king was not aware that the selection of Lord Edmond's township for the port was not the only option. I think it would be prudent to take the time to evaluate Lord Warin's claim, so I may report to the king that I did due diligence for all."

"Warin's region is leagues farther down the coast from the first port site," Arden protested.

"Yes," Orman replied, "but distance is not the only consideration. I understand that Lord Warin's region is significantly larger. I do not see any harm in judging for myself. Then all concerns will have been addressed once and for all."

Seanna gave her mother a look conveying that she knew they had been outmaneuvered, as Lord Warin leaned back in his seat with a gleam of satisfaction upon his face.

As the energy in the room dissipated, the men fell silent.

Dian rose to address Orman, her chin raised in defiance. "We can play Lord Warin's game for now, but the council's approval means nothing to me if it proves impossible to sway a man as rigid as he."

Warin shrugged his shoulders at the insult.

"Favoritism or not, we have the first right to the trade

agreements," said Dian. "If we leave, we take the favor of the king on our side. Are you willing to risk that?"

Lord Orman raised his hand in protest. "We can delay the outcome of this agreement for a short time. I will depart immediately with Lord Warin to his region to judge for myself and return with my conclusions. It is a good-faith mission, and I invite any other clansmen to accompany us on this journey."

Arden dropped his head into his hands, rubbing his temples, as Dian turned to leave the room. "Follow me," she ordered the Womara.

19

SECRETS REVEALED

The alliance council gathering ended in disarray after Lord Warin's insinuations. Lord Orman and Warin had already departed in haste from the hall, citing the need to prepare for the next morning's departure. Lord Stuart joined Lord Arden and added his voice to the fray, both men attempting to calm the frustrations of the councilmen who milled about, voicing their confusion.

Warin's allusion to the king's threat from his cousin and to his bond with Seanna had been effective enough to disrupt the day and plant seeds of mistrust. When all the women had departed, the men interjected words of dissent, incriminating the Womara and questioning their motives. The more outspoken clansmen directed their blame toward Lord Arden.

"You had prior knowledge of the Womara's advantage before this gathering?" one councilman barked.

"I knew a young woman had fallen in love, and I celebrated the news with her," Lord Arden answered. "I also respected Seanna's privacy, something that Lord Warin has besmirched with his accusations."

"And what of the prospect of gathering forces against the king from his cousin?" another councilman asked.

"What of it?" Arden snapped. "It is hearsay so far, and all the more reason for the alliance to move forward with the building of a port. We must have the ability to move ships and goods in any scenario that unfolds."

Lord Arden continued to stand his ground with Stuart at his side, calling for calmer heads as he attempted to control the spiraling breakdown of the day's events.

The council members called for the immediate formation of a coalition of men to journey with Lord Orman to Warin's southern region and be present at the evaluation of any port location there. The clansmen demanded that Lord Arden, Lord Stuart, or both be represented in the coalition but did not call for the same in the Womara's case.

Seanna followed her mother out of the hall with the entourage of Womara women. Once they were far enough away, Dian turned abruptly to face them. "This is lunacy," she said as she paced before the women.

Seanna watched the women exchange nervous looks as they stood silently; then Dian ordered, "Leave us for now. I will summon you later, when I have made some decisions."

The women departed, speaking softly to one another and shaking their heads. Seanna speculated that they must be in as much shock as she was, before Dian turned to her and said, "I think your instincts about Warin have proven him to be a poisonous snake."

"It is the fox Orman who is the poisonous snake," Seanna answered.

"Why?" Dian asked.

"Something is amiss, but I do not know what it is."

"Isn't Orman above such scrutiny? Did you not reveal to me that he was under the directive of the king to favor the Womara with this treaty?"

"Yes, but only Orman and I knew that," Seanna answered. "Warin only hinted at favoritism, and Orman allowed him to speak about it."

"So why does Orman move to pacify Warin, who is just a brute, blinded by his own ambition, and who, I suspect, still has a subversive desire to keep the Womara from the council?" Dian asked, clenching her fists.

"I do not know the purpose of such a diversion from an agreement that contained no surprises," Seanna answered, shaking her head. "But I do know that there is no such thing as a miscalculation for Lord Orman."

Dian sighed. "We must speak with Lord Arden. I am sure that he will summon us shortly to hear his private thoughts."

Seanna nodded. "It will be hard to be civil with my words after standing before those men today, under judgment once again."

"You should not be judged," Dian said, raising her voice. "I care not what these men think! But we will not underestimate any of their words or actions in the days that follow."

Across the courtyard, a servant stopped in his search and walked briskly toward them. "This is Lord Arden's summons," Dian predicted.

Seanna and Arden stood before the inert fireplace, listening to the questions that Dian posed as a chambermaid knocked softly upon the door, entering the private quarters to build an early-evening fire.

"What is the councilmen's temperament now?" Dian asked.

"They are confused and angry," Arden answered. "How did Warin manage, in such a short time, to disrupt and misdirect the outcome of the gathering?" He held up a hand to Dian and Seanna to pause as they stood silently, waiting for the maid to complete her task. Once she left, they continued their discourse.

"I blame myself for underestimating these men," Seanna said. "How could I have been so naive as to go through this scrutiny of my character a second time?" She turned to Lord Arden and added, "I should have advised you of the depth of Lord Orman's manipulative nature. My instincts tell me that we are dealing with the deceitfulness of both these men."

"I agree, and there can be no more conjecture," Dian said. "We must be vigilant. The stakes have changed in just a few hours."

"Surely this is not as dire as you predict," Arden said. "Warin may think he has a renewed opportunity to state once again his desire for a different port, but the council has already made its decision."

"Yes, but add Lord Orman to the fold, and it can be a perilous combination," Seanna answered. "I am unsure of his motives and how far he might go to impede the council's decision. I can caution you only about what my senses are telling me. I suggest you watch his every move."

Arden nodded. "The council decided to build the port in Lord Edmond's region, but the envoy's dictate could change that."

"And then we would be in danger of losing the rights to the port," Dian said.

"That should not happen," Seanna said. "The king told Lord Orman and me that the treaty favored both the Womara and the port of Lord Edmond. In truth, I never proposed the southern lands of Lord Warin for consideration when I familiarized the king with our regions."

"Why would you have? It is not under consideration," Arden said.

"What does Orman have to gain by diverting the signing of the treaty?" Dian asked.

"He is buying time," Seanna said, "though for what purpose, I do not know."

Arden turned to her with concern on his face. "Does Orman know your birthright? Did you tell James that you are my daughter?"

Seanna shook her head. "No one knows but us."

"At this juncture, that disclosure would only add fuel to the fire," Arden said. "And will you share your birthright with your king?"

"Maybe I should have before now, but I was unclear about my direction," Seanna admitted. "It has taken me time to reconcile myself to that knowledge. I do not know if it would change anything in the eyes of the king, but Lord Orman has never approved of our union and, I believe, has even worked covertly to prevent it."

"How so?" Dian asked.

Seanna clenched her fist at the memory of the day in the arena. "I believe even more strongly now that Orman wished to showcase my fighting skills with the king's guard, in front of James and his people, as a way both to humiliate me and to turn James's opinion of me if I failed."

"Warin will twist your new love, too," Arden said. "If he knows that Seanna could be the future leader of the Womara and it is revealed that she is my daughter, he will cast a dark net of complicity over us. A union between James and Seanna could ultimately mean a powerful divide between our northern and southern regions."

"That is premature. I do not need any more burden for the outcome of the alliance than I already bear," Seanna said.

"For now, let us focus on the journey at hand and push for a quicker resolution," Arden said. "I will heed your warning, Seanna, and keep a watchful eye out. I will accompany the coalition and take Lord Stuart with me."

"And what of the Womara?" Dian asked.

"In truth, I do not know if your presence will inflame the opposition more," Arden said. "And although it might be better to remain here, awaiting our return, I know you. You will not cower under their scrutiny."

"Nor will I be shunned," Dian said. "We cannot hide from Warin's insinuations. The threat of conflict is a rumor, and the love that James and Seanna bear for each other is a private matter. We must assume that the favoritism Lord Orman alluded to will not sway the council to exclude the Womara."

"Then you must travel with us," Arden said.

"Of course. These spiders will not be able to weave a greater web with our presence lingering over them," Dian answered.

"So be it, then," Arden answered.

"Seanna and I will depart with the coalition tomorrow," Dian said.

"No, I will not make the journey," Seanna replied, as Dian turned in surprise.

"You refuse? Will you give these men the satisfaction that they have beaten you back?" she demanded. The room seemed suddenly chilled as Dian stared at her, waiting for an answer. "What is the reason for your refusal?" Dian pressed, searching Seanna's face. "You hold something back, Daughter."

Seanna stood rigid and silent before her, biting her lip.

"You do not trust me," Dian said, stepping closer to her. "And maybe rightly so, for you might still harbor ill feelings over what you deemed my betrayal before."

"No, Mother. I have reconciled those feelings," Seanna answered. "But now I must ask that you trust me." Arden and Dian exchanged glances as she continued. "I need you to release Thea, Willa, and Ava from their service to you and allow them to accompany me. And, Lord Arden, I ask that you do the same for Gareth and Rand, from the alliance scouts."

Seanna knew that her request was bold, as her parents' puzzled expressions confirmed. "I am bound to silence, but you must not take it as defiance," she continued. "Father, you must trust me, too, on this." She bit her cheek to hold back her emotions.

"I do trust you. Come here, my child," Arden said.

Seanna stepped forward, and Arden placed his hands upon her shoulders, then drew her close and touched his forehead to hers, just as her mother did. She closed her eyes and tried to relax her tense shoulders as she felt the warmth of her father's breath upon her cheeks. They lingered for a few moments, heads touching, before they stepped apart and Seanna looked upon her father's face to see tears in his eyes.

She placed her hand upon her heart and bowed her head. "I have always been proud to pledge my allegiance to you as my lord, and I am now just as proud to call you my father."

Arden bowed his head to her.

"I shall leave tonight, but by the time you journey to Warin's region and return to the council, I will be back. That much I can tell you," Seanna said.

Orman sat quietly, listening to the prattling of Lord Arden's young chambermaid. He was already dressed in his nightclothes when he heard her soft knock on the door and invited her into his chamber.

"Milord, I would not have disturbed you at such an hour, but you told me to bring you anything I might hear that seemed worth repeating," she said.

"Of course—I did indeed tell you those very words. Come in and sit down. What is it that you have heard?"

"It is what I have seen and then heard that I think will interest you," she said. "I am sure that Lord Arden did not sleep alone last night."

Am I actually paying for this kind of frivolous information? Orman wondered, then asked, "Well, that is not so unusual, is it?"

"No, milord, but I think it might have been the leader of the women's clan who occupied his chambers."

Orman sat erect in his chair. "How do you know? Did you see them?" he pressed.

"No . . ." She hesitated. "But this evening I built a fire in his chambers. The woman and her daughter were there. When I left, no one noticed that the door was open slightly. I was able to listen for a short time outside in the shadows."

"Go on," Orman encouraged.

"They were speaking loudly about the gathering today and

what to do. I did not understand half their words or concerns, but I believe the young woman warrior is their child."

"How remarkable," Orman said, sitting rigidly but silently exclaiming, *Their child!*

"I had to force my hand over my mouth, milord, when Lord Arden asked if anyone knew that she was his daughter, and he and the woman leader vowed secrecy for now."

"What else?" he asked calmly.

"Only that the knowledge of her birthright would cause more trouble with the council."

So, Seanna, you are indeed much more than just a simple warrior, Orman reflected. *This information is priceless. If Seanna is the rightful heir of Lord Arden, then a union with the Womara would fortify two large regions and dominate the northern realm.*

"Was this what you were willing to pay me for, milord?" the maid asked, reminding him of his pledge.

Orman remembered the silver coins he had promised for anything she might overhear. "Indeed, my dear, and I will pay you handsomely, as I promised," he said, as he watched her face brighten. He pushed a small purse across the table. The maid smiled and took it, weighing the contents before pouring a few coins into her hands.

"These are yours," he offered, smiling. "But I must caution you, anyone who discovers these coins will question their origin and drive suspicion your way. Shall I hold the purse for you? You may take what you need anytime."

The maid could not take her eyes from the coins. "That is indeed wise, milord." She slowly placed the money back in the pouch but held out a single silver piece and placed it in her bodice.

"Be sure that you hide that well within your chamber," Orman said. "Even a few coins will draw the envy of your fellow servants."

"Yes, milord."

Orman rose, reaching for a decanter of wine on the shelf and lingering for a few moments while he poured them each a glass. "Let us drink to our new pact and your good fortune," he said. "I look forward to whatever additional information you may gather in my absence."

The maid smiled shyly, accepting the glass and raising it to her lips. Orman watched her drink the contents, studying her over the rim of his own goblet as he merely touched its edge to his lips. When she had finished, he said, "Well, it is late. I think that is enough excitement for one night."

"Thank you, milord," the maid said. She curtsied low and was turning to leave the room when Orman offered one more cautionary word.

"Good night, and remember that no one can know our secret."

"Yes, milord."

He watched her pull her shawl tightly around her shoulders as she disappeared down the dark hallway leading to the castle's back rooms and her bed. Orman sat down, throwing the contents of his glass into the fire and stroking his beard in thought. He presumed that the maid, once inside her small chamber, would have time to look around and hide her coin. She would lie down upon her bed, giddy with excitement over her good fortune, before the first, stabbing pain hit, doubling her body over as she drew her knees to her chest, trying to relieve the torment that felt like hot knives in her bowels and made her breath come in small gasps.

Lord Orman smiled to himself, wondering if a vision of his face would pass through her mind in those final moments when she realized that he had watched her drink her poisoned wine but had not emptied his own glass.

In the silent hours of the night, and in her last flickers of consciousness before eternal darkness descends, will she know she was betrayed?

He shrugged. *It is a shame to lose such a valuable informant, but it would have been only a matter of time before her tongue began to wag. I surmise that no one will question the death of a single chambermaid for long.*

Orman rose to wipe the glasses and replaced them to the shelf, pausing for a moment. *The stakes have certainly risen. A union between James and Seanna and the dominance of the northern realm would present a daunting impediment to my plans. Her bloodline must be challenged, even denounced, if possible. Does James know of it?*

Seanna left Arden and Dian standing alone as she moved quickly to seek out her traveling companions. She took a deep breath of night air as she walked briskly toward her chambers.

It is against my nature not to be forthright, she confessed to herself. *My only consolation is that soon, all will be revealed, for I grow tired of this concealment. In the meantime, however, I will not risk exposing my clandestine purpose.*

She entered her room and gathered her pack. *Only I can know that James arrives soon.* She and James had made their plans before she departed for home, agreeing that he would travel to her in one moon's time. They kept that decision secret, knowing that his council would have questioned the wisdom of such a move. A couple of days before his departure, he would present a proposal to travel to the new region and meet the leaders of the alliance, with the intended purpose of giving the new treaty his blessing.

James would inform his council that the agreement treaty should already be in place, based on the preliminary negotiations of their envoy. His presence in the new region would be worthy of a celebration, as well as a display of solidifying the goodwill between their realms. Seanna had questioned the safety of the journey, but he had deflected her concerns with encouraging words.

"I will not take chances, Seanna, and will offer no details beyond what is necessary. The royal ship I send by sea on the diplomatic mission will be a decoy, manned by Cedmon and my armed guard. They will depart at night, to favor the tide, and no one will see, confined to his quarters, a king who is indisposed with seasickness.

"A few of my most trusted guards and I will leave the day before, traveling by river to the peaks, and when the boat arrives at Lord Edmond's port, I should be safely on the other side of the mountain. I will have spies placed along the villages for a month in advance, to be active ears."

Seanna had concluded, *A journey by sea would be dangerous, especially if the king's cousin were to gain knowledge of his journey. But,* she had thought, *he will come over the pass.*

"I will be there when you climb the mountain," Seanna had vowed to him.

20

SEANNA WAITS

Fourteen Womara warriors and the alliance scouts Gareth and Rand camped at the base of the mountains, waiting for Seanna to return. She and Thea climbed the narrow trail alone, heading to the peaks near the pass, and had been out of sight for a full day.

Halfway up the mountain, Seanna paused to steady the horses and finally revealed to Thea their objective. "The king will come over the mountain pass," she said, as she watched Thea's eyes widen in surprise.

"I suspected," Thea confessed. "You must be overjoyed to see him."

"I am," Seanna said. "But I will not take a calm breath until I see his face and know that he is safe," she added, as she looked toward the mountaintop. "Everything was planned and in place before I left, but nothing could be revealed, to protect his safety."

"I understand the need for such secrecy," Thea answered. "And I see that it was important that Lord Arden, Stuart, and your mother left for Warin's region with the coalition. Their eyes and ears will be valuable and trustworthy, and the king will need their guidance if conflicts arise."

"Yes, it was necessary. Holding them back would have raised suspicions. I could not risk anyone discovering our diversion," Seanna answered.

"And you did not reveal your own plans, even to your mother?" Thea asked.

"Not even to her. I suspect that if Lords Warin and Orman concoct some diversion, it might reveal itself. She should be there if something unfolds in that region, or if any new hand is played in the treaty negotiations. My true fear is that Orman will learn of the king's presence and change his tactics."

"Then Lord Arden, Stuart, and your mother will be there," Thea said.

Seanna nodded. "The negotiations will be delayed for a short while. James wanted to see my world and meet my people. Now that he is here, he can facilitate the signing of the agreement and we can truly celebrate."

Thea smiled at her. "For now, let us celebrate the joy of his arrival."

Seanna said, "It is not the celebration we had planned, but it appears that his coming is timely, and a means to end the confusion and disruption among the alliance council. He will make short work of the diversionary tactics of Lord Warin and Orman if they are complicit," she said. "Someone as skilled as Orman will not make a false move even if he thinks that he is beyond the scrutiny of the king. We may see his true colors yet."

"Will you journey to the South when James comes?" Thea asked.

Seanna smiled. "No, to our forest first."

James and his men moved swiftly up the mountainside and on their second night camped at the site where his father had fallen in the ambush. As he sat alone in the twilight by a small fire, his heart ached a little less knowing that his father's body lay in his ancestral tomb in their city.

He spoke soft words to his father's spirit: "Father, a piece of your essence may still be bound to this place, but I hope that you are at peace. I think about you and my mother every day, and I miss you both desperately. I remember your words and guidance and strive to become a king who I hope will make you proud."

James regarded the darkening silhouette of the mountain peaks ahead and added, "Tomorrow we climb to the summit, and I will cross over the mountain pass to another place and into the arms of the woman I love. I cannot begin to tell you how extraordinary she is. I am very happy."

From his vest he drew a small piece of parchment with words written upon it and threw it into the fire's flames, watching the smoke curl upward into the night sky. His heart stirred at the thought of Seanna's smiling face. *I am almost there, my love.*

James wondered whether the ship's decoy had been effective; the boat would arrive in the port of Lord Edmond within a day. *The deception will draw any foul play toward that region.*

The risk to Cedmon and many of the king's young lords who served on his war council had weighed heavily on his mind since the plan's inception, but Cedmon had been unwilling to hear his concerns. "I have guarded you my whole life," he had said. "Do you think that I would agree to such a strategy if I did not draw the risk myself? I will rest easy once you are reunited with Seanna. I know you will be safe in her hands."

James had relented to his judgment.

"I will see you in this new land," Cedmon had said, flashing a rare smile as he escorted James to the large barge that would transport him down the river and toward the mountains. The boat was loaded with goods and manned by a small crew destined for the interior townships. James was concealed below, and the vessel drew no unusual inspection as it departed in the night, moving silently along the waterways.

In the dead of night, several miles beyond the outline of the city ramparts in the distance, the boat moored and ten of James's guards, dressed as common people, boarded. The horses were guided below the decks, and all weapons concealed. When the entourage stopped on the last riverbank the following day, the mountains were visible in the distance. Men and horses quickly unloaded, and the boat retreated silently down the river.

At first light, the men were ready and began their final ascent. Seanna had warned James that the last portion of the climb was hard, and the horses struggled to catch their footing in the crumbling rock as the guards gently urged them on. The band stood waiting as men with tracking skills scanned the barren peaks. James searched the jagged rocks anxiously, lifting his hand to shield his vision against the bright morning light, feeling his heart beating loudly against his chest.

In the distance, a movement caught his eye, and he let out a loud breath of relief. "There she is," he said, turning to his guard and pointing.

Over the last crest and among the craggy peaks stood Seanna

and another woman. She raised a hand in silent recognition as she moved to navigate the boulders, never taking her eyes off his. James's men remained behind him, letting him close the distance to her alone. Seanna jumped among the boulders, descending quickly to meet him.

As they rushed into each other's arms, James whispered, "My love, I cannot believe that you are finally here and that I can hold you once again."

Seanna leaned back to look deeply into his eyes, then kissed him passionately. "I can breathe again," she said, hugging him tightly at first but then pulling away, conscious of the men's stares.

They glanced sheepishly at each other before James drew her back to him, unconcerned. He kissed her slowly, savoring the taste of her lips, before letting her go and glancing up at the dark-haired woman who descended toward them.

Seanna took his hand and walked up the ridge. "James, this is my dearest friend, Thea, the Womara warrior who accompanied me. She is here for your protection."

Thea bowed her head with a hand on her heart. "Your Grace, it is a pleasure to meet you."

James smiled, searching Thea's dark eyes, comfortable under her unflinching gaze. *I see that the distinct stare of the Womara women is not a quality exclusive to Seanna.* He turned and beckoned his men to follow.

"Did all go well?" Seanna asked.

"I believe so," James answered. "When Cedmon arrives at Lord Edmond's port, he will share the purpose of the journey and our diversion."

Seanna nodded, before James pulled her close again, kissing her lightly and catching Thea's stare.

"You must forgive me," Thea said. "I am unaccustomed to seeing my friend in such a state."

Seanna laughed. "She teases me." She looked at the sun's position in the sky, then announced, "We must make haste. I have warriors awaiting our descent, and you will be more protected when we are farther within our valley. By nightfall, we will be deep in our forest."

"I cannot believe that I am here," James remarked, pulling Seanna closer again and touching his forehead to hers.

"You are here, my love," she replied.

The journey down the mountain trail was treacherous, and Seanna glanced around often to monitor James and his men's progress as they followed single file down the rocky path, their faces contorted with concentration on their footing. Thea escorted the rear of the group as they descended carefully.

"It is not much farther." Seanna voiced her encouragement as the men rested for a moment.

"I cannot believe that you ever climbed this trail and found the pass," James said.

"I have explored these peaks since I was a young girl," Seanna explained, and then confided, "I think that I was always destined to find it."

"And to find me as well," James said, smiling.

When the incline lessened to a manageable slope, Seanna moved ahead of the group to the waiting warriors at the bottom.

As James and the men traveled the last several hundred yards and gathered at the bottom of the trail, Gareth whispered to Seanna, "Is that who I think it might be?"

Several of James's men turned to view their path and stood to shake their heads in wonderment at their accomplishment. "Your Grace, please tell us we will not be going back over that pass on our return," one said, as nervous laughter broke out among them.

James laughed, too, before turning his attention to the other warriors standing together.

Seanna stepped closer to her group and announced, "This is King James, of the city of Bathemor. I have pledged him our protection."

All of the women warriors bowed their heads in unison, placing their hands over their hearts, and Gareth stepped forward, bowing low. "Your Grace, I am Gareth, of the alliance scouts. I serve the alliance and Lord Arden." With a sweeping gesture of his hand, he motioned for Rand and the remaining alliance scouts to step forward.

"We also pledge you our protection, Your Grace," Rand said on their behalf.

James smiled. "Thank you all. I accept your service."

Seanna said, "We will ride to our valley and tonight shall be within the forest, where you will be our welcome guests. We will rest a couple of days before we continue our travels."

All of James's men nodded, as their king replied, "I think a respite will be welcome for everyone."

"Good," Seanna said. "Let's move."

It was near dusk when the band dismounted and led their horses to the pathways that entered the darkening forest ahead. Torches lit the route, casting looming shadows in the half-light. Some of the king's men squinted into the shadowy recesses of the forest; others looked up to the canopies where sentries stood, silently watching them, backlit by small torches.

Seanna walked at James's side. "It can be disquieting to walk into the darkening shadows of the deep forest," she acknowledged. "It touches our primal fears, but we have made this our home for many generations."

James sensed his trepidation as the trees closed around him, but just then, the interior of the forest grew brighter. As they approached the township, illuminated by its evening lamps, the men stopped, eyes wide. They looked around at the center portion, built within the cleared forest floor, and at the flickering lanterns of the shops and homes radiating outward and interspersed with the tall trees that surrounded them.

"This is amazing," James exclaimed. "It is unlike anything I have ever seen, yet it is exactly the way you have described it to me."

Seanna grinned at his words and stopped to address the men. "We have quarters for you, and I will refresh the guard of your king. Enjoy a night of rest, and explore our town."

"Is there a tavern?" one man asked, as the others laughed.

"There is," Seanna said with a laugh. "Rand will settle you in your rooms and then guide you there, if you wish." Next, she signaled Willa and Ava to her side. "Pick your guards and post a radius around my house."

When all the instructions had been handled to her satisfaction, she dismissed her warriors and took James's hand. "Let me show you my home."

They followed a well-worn path from the township until it diverted onto a narrower trail leading to the steps of her house, built into a bank covered with cascading ferns. Seanna's small cottage stood nestled against a towering tree. James paused to admire a large wood carving of an owl, wings spread, above her door.

"My totem," she explained, smiling.

Seanna opened the door and moved into the darkened interior as James stood in the doorway, watching her light the lamps. As the room brightened with their glow, he admired the simple but comfortable-looking rooms.

The centerpiece of the space was the hearth, built upon rock slabs and fitted with irons for cooking. Around the ledge was an elaborate, ceiling-height spiral mosaic design of many different-colored rocks.

A large chair sat alongside the fireplace, as well as a table with chairs for eating. On the opposite side of the room was the kitchen, with pantry shelves well stocked with jars and bottles of various shapes and sizes. Against a far wall stood a bookshelf made from the curved limbs of trees, housing many volumes contained by bookends made of polished rock. A small desk with writing papers, quills, and ink well fit snugly underneath a window; a vase upon it held the feathers of a variety of birds.

Seanna opened the door to a back room, lighting the candles within. On an elevated floor, a large bed, covered in a blanket woven of many richly colored textiles, was placed near a window that opened into the forest.

Seanna discarded her weapons, crossing the room to close the door behind them. James reached for her and pressed her against the wall, kissing her passionately, as they fumbled urgently to remove their clothes. He caught his breath while he unbuttoned the clasps of her tunic, pulling her shirt down to her waist, and Seanna tugged his shirt over his shoulders and crushed her naked chest against his.

James lifted her in his arms, and she wrapped her legs around his waist as he carried her to the bed. He lowered Seanna upon the woven coverlet, pushing up her long skirt, exposing her bare legs and running his hands along her downy thighs. He struggled to get his pants off, unwilling to take the time to remove his boots.

Seanna reached out to draw him down to her and gasped as he entered her deeply, causing them both to moan with pleasure. When Seanna arched her back against him, James moved slowly, trying to restrain himself, but Seanna grasped him hard and with her movements made him lose control. They cried out in unison at their climaxes. James had to catch his breath and steady his senses before moving from her and collapsing at her side.

He smiled sheepishly, and they both began to laugh. "Well, that was short but very satisfying," he confessed.

"Fortunately, that was just the first round," she said, rolling off the bed. She stood before him and slowly removed all of her clothing, letting James watch her undress before she knelt to remove his boots and leggings. They made love passionately for the next several hours until finally, exhausted and satiated, lying naked on the bed, they rested, listening to the sounds of the forest through the open window.

Seanna ran her fingers down James's chest, following the line of hair to his manhood as he lay smiling with his arms resting over his head. She brought her fingers to rest upon the leather tie around his neck with the moonstone hanging from it.

"I have never taken it off, as I promised you," he said.

"It is a stone of powerful protection," Seanna answered. "And tomorrow we will venture into the forest to fulfill its purpose."

"How can a stone have a purpose?"

"Tomorrow I will tell you."

"What are our plans, my love? You have spoken only of the

forest. We will not journey to Lord Arden's region tomorrow?" James asked.

"No, there has been a delay," Seanna explained, as she saw his questioning expression. "But let me postpone the telling of details for now so that we can have this one evening free of the talk of politics. I want to share my home with you."

Seanna stood before the fire in a nightdress, the light from the flames defining her body through the cloth as she warmed a small meal at her hearth. James watched her from his chair, drinking the glass of wine she had offered. He could not take his eyes off her. *I love the way she looks in her shift*, he thought. The neckline opened seductively while exposing her bare breasts underneath. Her hair, undone from its braid, was wild and tousled about her face.

"I could sit here and watch you all night," James said, making Seanna smile.

She smiled and answered, "I would take you to the hot springs tonight, but, in truth, I am reluctant to leave this tranquil moment."

"Let us stay here, then." James reached for her hand, leaning forward to smell her fingertips before kissing them. "I wish to be enveloped in your scent. How much I have missed that."

Seanna looked down shyly.

"I can still find words that make you blush," he said.

"You say things that are unfamiliar to my ear," she said softly, "but the sweetness of your words makes my heart soar."

"I cannot express how comforted I am to see your beautiful face before me," James confessed. "I have had many dark thoughts of late, and without you to comfort me, it has been difficult."

"What such thoughts?"

"Nightmares, almost. I have been dreaming that I arrived at the empty mountaintop and stood there alone because you never came." He watched her brow furrow with concern. "Or I was lost in the mist of the peaks, wandering and searching for a way back to you."

"Those dark dreams are over, for I am here," Seanna said. "But I, too, have suffered from our parting."

"How so, my love?"

"I never understood when others spoke of a physical pain caused by separation from their loved ones. But now I understand that feeling of anguish."

He drew her onto his lap and held her close. In the predawn hours, they finally fell into a deep sleep, wrapped in each other's arms, unwilling to let go.

21

THE DEEP FOREST

James woke to the sounds of chirping birds in the tree branches outside Seanna's open window and of cupboards opening and closing in the pantry. He stretched his arms overhead and rolled onto his side to look out at the morning light filtering through the forest.

Seanna entered the room and came to his side. "Good morning."

James beamed. "How wonderful to wake to the sounds of the birds and the sight of your beautiful face."

Seanna sat down on the edge of the bed while looking out the window. "It is such a simple thing, isn't it? These carefree little creatures calling to each other and heralding the day always brings me joy. However, you must get up soon," she added, and laughed when James frowned at the prospect. "I have already met with your men and my guards and informed them that we will be gone for a day."

"Are you always this serious in the morning?" James asked as she stood.

"Only this morning. I have some food laid out for us. Let's eat before we leave."

James sighed. "If I must." He sat up, rubbing the sleep from his eyes. "Where are we going?"

"It is not a place that I can describe. You must experience it for yourself."

"All right," he said, looking up at her. "But I sense that you wish to talk?"

"Yes, I told you there were happenings that I needed to share," Seanna answered, and her words sobered his mood. "I want to tell you about the aftermath of the alliance council gathering and some unexpected revelations that may concern you."

James rose, suddenly fully awake. "What has happened?"

For the next hour, they sat and ate the modest meal that Seanna had set out as she told him everything that had transpired at the gathering of the council and about the turn of events that had diverted the treaty discussions. Several times during her discourse, James left his chair to pace the small room.

"I did not plan for this outcome!" he barked. "Why would Orman initiate such an act that required traveling to this Lord Warin's region to evaluate a port location against my wishes?"

"Do you think that it is a sincere act on his part to consider Warin's region?" Seanna asked.

"Not if your council has already deemed the region not viable," James answered. "But without discussing his reasoning with him directly, I cannot ascertain whether is it a merited diplomatic maneuver. I intend to ask him when I see him."

"I think that his motivations are clouded at this moment," Seanna said. "And it is good fortune that you are here to settle the matter."

"Why is he clouded?" James asked.

"Lord Warin's words might have swayed him. I have spoken before with you about this lord of the South. He is not a friend to the Womara. In addition to asking for the port to be considered in his region, Warin further disrupted the gathering to reveal the treachery of your cousin and the king who now gives him sanctuary. He implied that a threat from across the sea loomed over you and could influence the alliance's negotiations."

"In what way?" James asked. "That treachery is common enough knowledge, and I have asked for no pledge to arms."

"I am afraid that I cannot offer you any greater insights, though Warin implied that our union swayed the decision about the port in the Womara's favor."

"And why should it not if I want it so?" James asked, raising his voice. "I owe you my life."

Seanna took his hands in hers. "I do not think of it that way. Maybe it will be a fortuitous venture to let Orman evaluate Warin's region, so no doubts exist about the best location. Should I have told you of this before I returned home?"

"No, because a different port does not serve you and your clan, and it appears that I will have the backing of the alliance. I do not need more," he said, rising from his chair. "After our stay in the forest, we must travel to Lord Edmond's township the day after tomorrow. Cedmon is there with my guards, awaiting my command. Can we send word for the coalition and Lord Orman to meet us in Arden's township?"

"Yes, I think we should return to Lord Arden's region," Seanna said. "There, you can stand before the entire alliance council."

"True," James said, "and I will pledge and sign the treaty

myself." He sighed. "Are we ever to have a moment of peace to ourselves?"

"Soon, I hope."

They left quietly, with only the packs on their backs, and traveled deep into the interior of the forest. To James's untrained eye, they followed no determinable trail. Seanna told him that she used natural landmarks—trees, boulders, or water sources— to guide her through this terrain that she had known since she was a child.

He tried to track their path with visual references to stave off the disorientation he felt once they passed the perimeter of her village, but soon surrendered to following Seanna's steady steps. He could only estimate the time of day by the movement of the sun in places where it penetrated enough to cast a shadow upon a tree. The vegetation grew thick and varied, and he frequently stopped to comment on plants that were unlike anything that he had seen before in his own woods. "I feel like I am in a different world," he said, as Seanna only smiled.

The farther they hiked into the interior, the more rugged and steep the terrain became. Large boulders buttressed banks covered with moss, and ferns clung to the crevices. Ancient trees towered over them; others, which had toppled, exposed their gnarled roots and were large enough for someone to crawl inside for shelter.

"Exactly how deep are we going?" James finally asked.

"We are close," Seanna replied.

They climbed through a canyon where water descended over stones from the rock walls and collected in a small, emerald-green pool. They stopped to rest and drink the cold, crystal-clear water.

A few yards away stood a grove of trees, and on one of the trunks was carved the face of a nature god.

James turned in surprise to Seanna. "Is this it?"

She nodded. "I marked it as a place containing the living spirit of our clan."

A thick bed of ferns covered the entire ground, and only thin rays of sunlight could penetrate the heavy canopy above. It looked like a cathedral to James, and he felt the deep stillness that permeated other majestic places of worship he had known.

Here, one does not need to kneel, head bowed in silent prayer. The sacredness of the surrounding forest calms all the senses.

The sounds of birds became more distant, and even though he knew there were still several hours of daylight left, the forest shadows darkened around them. Seanna stood at the center of the grove for a moment with her eyes closed and breathing deeply. "I was here during my rite of passage," she said.

"How old were you when you had your rite?"

"It is always after a girl's first blood—the transition time when a young Womara becomes a woman and a warrior."

James looked around at the changing shadows on the trees, as his eyes adjusted to the darkening twilight. "How long did you have to stay in these woods alone?"

"I am not sure. I lost count of the days."

"Were you not afraid?"

"At times I was, but facing fear is the way of the Womara warrior and survival is a mandate of my people. Everything I had learned up to that point in my life was tested during my time here."

"What happened?"

"I had been within the forest for many days, but in my foraging I had not found any substantial food yet."

"You were suffering?" James asked.

"For a time. I grew weak and knew I must find something soon." Seanna glanced around her. "But when I rested in this place, I found that I was not alone."

"What do you mean?"

James searched her face as Seanna said, "Let me try to explain. I had scavenged most of the day and rested in this very spot of the grove. I laid my head upon my arms and might have slept for a moment. When I looked up, she was there."

"Who?" James asked.

"I do not know who she was, but a woman stood looking at me. She wore the clothes of a warrior dressed for battle and held a small sword and shield."

James inhaled sharply.

"Her hair was a brilliant red and fanned around her face, almost like flames. Her eyes were illuminated and a brilliant green."

"By the gods," James swore, drawing his knees to his chest to ward off the chill that ran through his body.

"I knew it was a vision because I could see the tree through her body behind her. My blood chilled when I sensed that she was not of this world. I remember thinking that I must be starving, until she spoke to me and I rose in fear."

"She spoke to you?"

"Yes," Seanna replied. "'You are of my blood,' the apparition said, as she pointed her sword at me. 'There is nothing here that can harm you, and nothing that you cannot defeat. Have courage.'

"I could not answer her," Seanna continued. "Then she turned to walk into the forest but stopped before a thicket and looked back at me. 'Bring back to me what is mine,' she demanded, before she faded into the trees."

James stared at Seanna, unable to speak.

Seanna continued, "Where she disappeared into the forest, I discovered a small rabbit with a broken leg, trying to drag itself into the bush. I thanked her for the gift and the animal for its sacrifice and killed it quickly with my knife. I drank some blood to restore myself."

James grimaced. "And the woman?"

"Gone. I was alone again but no longer afraid."

James shivered involuntarily. "I am chilled just thinking of such an encounter. How could you not question your rationality?"

"I did, and judged my terror also. But when I had calmed, I knew that I had passed through the other side of my fear, and I felt strengthened," Seanna answered.

"Who do you think she was?"

"She is the guardian spirit of our forests. She and the others."

"Others?" James asked.

"All the woman who died the day of our great battle. Their bodies returned to the forest, and I believe that their spirits are here, deep within these places." Seanna looked around at the trees. "And I am here to fulfill a vow and return to my ancestor a part of that spirit."

They sat in silence for a few moments. James's hand drifted to the stone that hung around his neck, and he rubbed its smooth contours. "Does this place have something to do with this stone?" he asked. "You told me that you would share its story."

Seanna nodded. "Remember that I gave it to you when we were standing on the dock before my departure for home?"

"You told me, 'I have something for you,'" James recounted. "And when you opened your hand, there lay the stone, with a small hole chiseled in it, strung through with a leather thong."

"You asked what it was," Seanna answered, "but I told you only to wear it and keep it close to your heart—and to bring it to me when you came over the pass."

"I felt as if the stone protected me," James said.

"Yes, I think so. It was a gift given to me by an old woman in the marketplace of your city a few days before I was to depart for my home."

James raised an eyebrow.

"She approached me, asking for a moment of my time. In her hand she held the stone that hangs on your necklace. 'What is this?' I asked her. Her next words sent a chill down my spine: 'This stone has been in my family for many years,' she said. 'It belonged to my ancestors.'

"'And why would you offer it to me, old one?' I asked.

"She grinned widely, showing gums that contained only a few teeth. She retold the tale of a world beyond the mountains and clan of women to whom her ancestor owed his life. He said that one day someone from that clan would come, and that whoever was the first should be the one to have the stone."

James touched the talisman again.

"Her eyes were clouded by age but shone with an inner light after she spoke," Seanna went on. "Then the old woman stepped closer and pressed the stone into my hand. She shared, 'My ancestor told us that contained within the stone was the essence of his heart, and that we must return his spirit to this place beyond the mountains, where he would find again the one he had loved.'"

"Who was this man?" James asked.

"The old one told me that his name was Landon and that his home, and hers, was a valley at the base of the far mountains," Seanna said. "I could not disguise my shock when she spoke his name. I knew it well from my past; it is a name from my line of people. If it be the same man, Landon was my great-great-grandfather."

James's eyes went wide. "Then we share a common origin, your people and mine?"

"I am not certain. The old woman offered only that she had to make the journey to honor her ancestor's wishes when she heard that a warrior woman had come from across the mountains. I asked that she bring her family the next day and share the location of her home, but she never returned. I had no time to journey to find her valley, because I left by sea and not through the mountain pass."

"Do you think the story is true?" James asked.

"I judged her words to be sincere. Who could know the name of my ancestor? I was a stranger in your land."

"Do you remember my delight when you placed it around my neck?" James asked. "You said that the stone bound us together."

Seanna nodded.

"I did not understand the meaning then, but now I think I do," he said. He removed the necklace and handed it to Seanna. She wrapped it in a cloth, before placing it in a small box. She rose and dropped to her knees to dig a hole with her knife at the base of the great tree where the woman's spirit had first appeared. She buried the contents and bowed her head, placing her hand on her heart.

"May this bring you peace."

James shivered again, and when Seanna rose, he reached out to her. "Come close and comfort me," he said. "I feel the spirits that surround us."

Seanna sat down beside him. "I think that you shiver because you feel something greater at play here."

"What do you mean?"

"You and I have been moving through life on paths that I cannot fully describe, except to say that I feel as if these paths are merging and drawing us closer while pieces of our fate fall in place."

"I have felt it since the day we met," James acknowledged.

"In this place that is so sacred to me, I will share my last truth with you—a secret that only Lord Arden and my mother, Dian, know."

James gazed into her eyes, waiting.

"I have learned that Lord Arden is my birth father. He revealed the truth in a letter he wrote to my mother before I left for the mountains to reunite with you. My father felt that it was time to share that I was their child."

"The great lord is your father?"

Seanna nodded. "Yes. At the time, I was in shock about such a revelation. I could not come to terms with my birthright, and I therefore did not share this news with you."

James thought for a moment, before replying, "You are the destined leader of your people, and possibly much more now that he has revealed that you are his daughter."

"I don't feel that way," Seanna confessed. "I am only what you see before you—a simple warrior who wishes to remain so."

"I think that destiny has a different path in mind for you."

"For *us*." Seanna smiled as she took his hands in hers. "I will not sacrifice my heart for anything that is not my choice. From this point forward, I want to shape our course together."

James leaned forward and kissed her deeply. "When I return, will you come back with me?"

"Yes, I will." Seanna rested her back against a tree, then pulled James against her chest and enfolded him in her arms to warm him as they stared into the fire. "I love you," she whispered in his ear.

22

ALL PATHS MERGE

Lord Orman stood upon the bluffs overlooking Lord Warin's township. He braced himself against the offshore winds of the coast that buffeted him and the coalition members as they gazed along the coastline from the high vantage view.

Upon their arrival the day before, Lord Warin had wasted no time in initiating an outing through his region, starting with this morning's gathering. The coalition, composed of Lord Arden, Stuart, Dian, and several high-ranking clansmen of the alliance council, was present and stared down the predominantly barren coastline and its miles of wooden barrier wall constructed as a main line of defense. The fortification stood at least ten feet high and was manned by sentries in towers every half mile.

Orman watched the coalition members' faces observing the blockade along the coastline but could not discern their assessments from their expressions.

"As you can see, our defense is strong enough to secure a hundred miles of coast," Warin boasted.

"Not from fire, Lord Orman," Dian said, and Orman noticed Warin glower at the criticism. When Dian turned away to speak to Lord Arden, Orman overhead her words: "What a soulless place! Not a tree for miles; the land stripped to build this abomination."

Orman wondered why Seanna was not present, but when he had posed the question to Dian, feigning concern about her absence, Dian had dismissed his query with only a curt statement that Seanna was not needed on the journey and had chosen to remain behind.

Her words rang false. Did she seek to protect Seanna from any more humiliation? Unlikely—the Seanna I know would not display such weakness. So where is she?

Orman's thoughts returned to the vista before them, and he had to admit to himself that he agreed with Dian's assessment of the barrier. The region was sprawling but looked dull and barren. The township itself, encircled by an outer wall of tall wooden poles with sharpened points, felt more like a prison to him than a thriving community.

The area lacked vibrancy, stripped of the local fauna and nearby forests over the many years it had taken to build such a defense against invaders by sea. He thought he understood the vulnerability that drove men to construct such barriers, but it was still an eyesore.

The region was strategically larger than Lord Edmond's but fundamentally flawed as the most viable option for a port. A good portion of the land to the far south lay surrounded by tidal flats too shallow for the safe anchoring or mooring of ships. Lord Edmond's region had a deep natural harbor that could provide that safety, as well as the potential for expansion to create a man-made port for receiving ships and transferring cargo. It would take a great deal of manpower to enhance a harbor where boats could anchor safely here.

Now I understand why Warin is so eager for the alliance council's endorsement; they have the resources to supply his region with more of the necessary men and materials to expand, Orman realized. But without a bay or a long strait, anchored ships would not be protected against the waves and winds that ravaged the shoreline, and he could see no large river mouth that could provide more places to anchor or dock goods.

Warin's region could, at best, possibly be used as a smaller, secondary port if products need to be moved farther down the coast. But I also agree with Dian that the barrier on which Warin so prides his region is vulnerable to fire.

"I think we have seen enough from this viewpoint," Orman finally announced. *Warin's hopes will be dashed when I disclose that this cannot be a location for primary commerce, and it will be difficult to promote continued optimism while I try to anticipate my next move. He will be a hard man to dissuade; I will need to offer something of greater value to appease him if I wish to keep him as an ally.*

Orman made overtures of dispatching his surveyors and mappers immediately to the task of evaluating the waterways, and that seemed to satisfy Warin, but his engineers' wary glances told him the same thing he had already surmised for himself: *No port will be built here.*

Orman drew a measure of relief from knowing that Warin's unsuitable territory made it easier to concur with the king's decree that the port be built in Lord Edmond's region. He had never seriously considered opposing the king's wishes, nor was he tempted by Warin's offer to be the port master. This diversion had garnered what he needed: a covert opportunity to gain a good perspective of the lands from north to south. He could now offer Thomas this important geographical knowledge to bolster his value as a resource. Any more delays or digressions would risk opening him to greater scrutiny and suspicion. *I may have compromised the council's view of me, but I will restore their goodwill as soon as possible.*

He felt the Womara leader watching his every move and knew he had made an adversary of her through his silence amid Warin's accusations. *Dian is on her guard, and for good reason. It will be more challenging to sway her back to my side.* But he smiled to himself as he thought of the valuable information the maid had given him. *I can hold that knowledge of Seanna's birth close and, when the time is right, use it against both Dian and Lord Arden.*

James and Seanna, escorted by his men and the Womara warriors, had traveled for two days and set up camp for the evening. When she and James had returned from the forest's interior, Seanna had immediately summoned the guard to her. "We must travel soon," she announced. "Prepare yourself, for we leave in the next hour."

She added quietly to James, "I will feel more at ease when we reach Lord Edmond's township. We must unite with your guard and travel on to the alliance council."

James tried to lighten her mood: "I do not want you to worry. I feel safe with you and your people."

"My thanks," Seanna said, placing her hand over her heart.

"I am only sorry that we must leave your home so soon."

Seanna hugged him and said, "When all this is done, we shall return."

James moved among his men as they settled into their camp at the end of a long day of travel on horseback. Before he returned to his fire with Seanna, he wanted to know their thoughts on the lands they had passed through. He sat back to watch as a few of the men joined the Womara warriors' fires, and smiled at the animated conversations he overheard. *There are some among my men who might feel like I did when I met these women for the first time.*

James observed Rand sitting among the Womara, with some of the alliance men at his side. When Seanna joined him, he said, "My men are curious about Rand's having been raised among the Womara and all women."

"Have they found that it has made him less of a man?" Seanna asked.

"No, they speak highly of him."

"As they should. He is thoughtful and well respected among the alliance scouts," Seanna added.

"I understand that Willa is his mother," James said. "I saw them speaking in earnest many miles back when we rested near a grove."

Seanna nodded. "She is. She might have shared with him that we passed through the area where a raiding tribe abducted her many years ago."

James gasped. "I did not know!"

"She was held captive for almost a year in the far North and escaped only after killing her captor, whose child she was carrying."

"Escaped and journeyed back to your forest alone?" James asked.

"Yes, and she gave birth along the way within the hollow of a tree, then carried the baby for weeks to return home."

"My God!" James exclaimed. "What an ordeal to survive."

"Indeed, but we are strong," Seanna answered.

The laughter of the group by the fire drew James's attention as he sat thinking. "It is still such a remarkable idea for me that all of your women are so individually and collectively empowered."

Seanna surveyed the group, smiling proudly.

"Is the young warrior beside him his woman?" James asked.

"*His* woman? I do not think that is the right description," she chided.

"I meant no offense."

"I know," Seanna said, her tone softening. "You see with new eyes every day, and I am grateful for your openness. But in truth, I do not know the answer to your question. They have grown up together, and I feel that they represent our future," Seanna answered.

"Why the future?"

"Because they have been raised in true equality."

James shook his head. "Equality between men and women—still a difficult concept for many, including me, to understand at times."

"That is an honest enough answer for now."

"Can there ever be a real balance?" James asked. "Men will always seek dominance and have sought power over others since the beginning of time."

"Yes, but men have also risen to fight oppression and then, sadly, become the oppressors themselves. It will take a greater force to change their will," she replied.

"Is the way of the world not set?" James asked.

"Nothing is set," Seanna remarked. "My grandmother Landra did not stop to ask anyone if we could do anything—she demanded that it must be."

James nodded.

"Thea and I are of a generation of women who fear what could be lost in giving ourselves to men. Thea asked me when I returned what I could ultimately sacrifice by falling in love with a man so different from us."

James shifted toward her as she continued, "But I could not answer her. I can say only that you are a different man in the world of men, and that makes me love you more."

James reached out and touched her face gently.

"My mother once told me that loving a man who embraces you as a true partner is the balance. Spend time with Rand, and you may understand what I mean."

James nodded. "I will. I want to understand. I have returned from the forest with you, and I feel transformed."

"Your words give me chills," Seanna said, rubbing her arms and settling closer to him.

In the late afternoon of the following day, the travelers dropped over the rise to view Edmond's township, nestled around a blue-green bay. The king's ship was moored within the harbor, its purple flags fluttering in the wind.

My men are here! James rejoiced.

Seanna's smile reassured him that they had reached their destination. She sent a Womara ahead to announce their arrival, and when they approached the outer boundary, Cedmon stood waiting with his guards behind him.

James spurred his horse ahead and dismounted before his men as Seanna rode up. "Cedmon!" James shouted.

Cedmon grinned. "Your Grace, I am relieved to see that you are safe!"

Cedmon greeted Seanna as she walked her horse toward him. "My lady, it is comforting to see you at the side of my king."

"And you, Cedmon. Welcome to our lands!" she exclaimed.

"Lord Edmond anxiously awaits your arrival, Your Grace. Let us escort you into town."

James nodded, but before he could mount, Cedmon asked, "May I speak with you in private before we reach the lord's hall?"

"Let us hold here for a moment so that you can tell me what you wish to share," James said. "Your journey. Any problems?"

"None on the journey, and the decoy worked very well, but I bear unwelcome news that I received right before my departure," Cedmon said.

"What is it?"

Cedmon leaned closer and spoke quietly: "Word was received that Thomas has proven resourceful and has secured a pledge of alliance with King Havlor."

"Of course. Was that not expected of Thomas?" James asked.

"It was, Your Grace," Cedmon answered. "But Thomas has solidified that pledge by marrying King Havlor's daughter."

James stopped short. "He has married?"

"It will be a great strategic union and a powerful alliance with the northmen," Cedmon continued.

"What could this mean?" James asked.

"It could have far-reaching impact beyond the barbarians' borders. It is an opportunistic move for these raiders. If they intend to pursue invasion to secure more lands, then no realm to the north is safe, and his union will cast a long shadow over our lands, too. Thomas's marriage has provided a reason to return his bloodline to the throne," Cedmon explained. "And he is enboldened in this pact, the spies report."

"I imagine that Thomas has offered our lands and trading port as the prize," James answered, shaking his head.

"The betrayal of your own blood must feel acute, as Thomas seeks to exploit the closeness of your childhood, thinking he understands your weakness," Cedmon said.

"He is hoping for vulnerability," James said, standing taller. "But he no longer knows the man I have become. We will not lose everything we hold dear to his blind ambition, or to the brutes he has bedded with."

Orman had allocated several days for his surveyors to map Lord Warin's coastline and summarize their conclusions. He grew bored with the wait, and after the evening meal on the third night, as he endured the usual stares from Dian across the room, he thought, *I have grown tired of her, too.*

She and Arden had been very careful in all their interactions. To the uninformed eye, they appeared as allies united in a common goal, not as the lovers he knew them to be.

And what of your ambitions, Dian, for your clan and your daughter? When will you play your hand?

Warin had pressed Orman privately for his evaluation, but Orman had intimated that when the surveyors were finished, they would journey back to Arden's region, where he would disclose his findings before the entire alliance. *All I must do is maintain this ruse for a while longer so that we can return to the council.*

Warin had turned sullen at Orman's words, but he had not challenged Orman in the coalition's presence. As Orman had left to return to his quarters, he had noticed a lone rider galloping through the town's gates and dismounting before the guest quarters.

Later that evening, Orman heard a knock on his door. *This cannot be Lord Warin!*

The person knocked again. "Lord Orman, it is Dunstan. May I have a moment?"

Orman opened the door to find Warin's nephew standing before him. "My lord, forgive my intrusion, but I need to speak with you."

Orman stepped outside the door to view the corridor before he allowed Dunstan to enter. "Is this wise?"

"I have news that might be of great importance to you," Dunstan said.

"Where is your uncle? Or have you already brought this information to him? Did he send you to convey it to me?"

"No, my lord, my uncle knows nothing of this," Dunstan replied. "This news may be of greater worth to you than to him at this time."

Orman felt uneasy, though he was unsure of the source of his discomfort, as he poured them both a glass of wine. Dunstan accepted his goblet and drank the contents in one quaff.

"Speak, man," Orman ordered.

"One of my spies arrived this afternoon from Lord Edmond's township."

"Yes?"

"I have been most fortunate to secure eyes and ears that give me information even within Lord Edmond's court," Dunstan boasted.

Yes, you have an admirable talent, Orman thought.

"My spies reported that your king's ship has been moored for many days in Lord Edmond's harbor."

Orman stopped the glass of wine at his lips, a chill running down his spine. "What do you mean? Was the king on it?"

"I do not think so, my lord. It appears that the ship bears the king's man Cedmon, but not the king himself."

"For what purpose?" Orman asked, as he felt a renewed chill down his spine.

"Could the king have sent Cedmon to Lord Edmond's region to assess your progress with the treaty?"

Orman did not answer, only stared back at him.

"My sources are very reliable and report that Cedmon remains as a guest of Lord Edmond," Dunstan continued. "They also tell me that within Edmond's court, the older lord clandestinely prepares for the arrival of the king himself."

My God! Orman held his breath, and his stomach gripped at the news. *This is why Seanna did not fight hard enough against the accusations hurled at her and is not here with the coalition. The ship is a decoy. She has left to meet him. James must be coming through the mountain pass!*

Orman felt Dunstan's eyes following his movements while he paced around his chambers, trying to think.

"You are not pleased with the prospect of the king's man, or maybe even your king, arriving?" Dunstan asked.

"The news, if true, has caught me unaware. I know nothing of the king's reasons for traveling here," Orman answered.

"That must be something that you are unaccustomed to, my lord," Dunstan said, smirking.

"And why did you bring this to me and not your uncle?" Orman asked.

"As I said, I thought it had more worth to you than to him. And you may want to delay the coalition's knowledge of this information."

"How long can this remain quiet?" Orman wondered. "Your uncle would certainly judge your move insolent and disloyal. Why would you risk his wrath?"

Dunstan poured himself more wine. "By now, you should be well accustomed to my uncle's shortcomings. He lacks the subtlety and discipline of a man willing to delay immediate gratification, and his relentless desire for power often blinds him. For example, he cannot see that you have only feigned an interest in our region for the port since your arrival. It is obvious to all that the location is not suitable."

"I have not made my final determination," Orman said.

"Haven't you? I do not know the reason for your delay, but I think that you have used my uncle as a pawn to play against the alliance."

"He is a pawn only if I have something to gain from it."

"If your king has arrived, will it not force your hand?" Dunstan asked.

Orman sat back in his chair, evaluating the question. *I do not yet know how clever you are, Dunstan, but my instincts tell me I should not underestimate you.* "What are you proposing?" he asked.

"The council is already suspicious of my uncle's dissent. He has always been regarded as opportunistic and self-serving, and, as you have experienced, he is not above acting covertly to undermine the alliance. I fear at times that he takes us down a dark path with his greed and his desire to win at all costs," Dunstan mused.

"And you wish to change this possible outcome?"

"Warin is childless, and I am his next of kin and will be the leader when the time comes. I am not without my own aspirations, and that forces me to be tolerant of my uncle's volatile nature and his self-absorbed temperament."

"What is that to me?" Orman asked.

"I am not sure of your own objectives, Lord Orman, but you may have need of an alliance with a more like-minded leader in the future," Dunstan offered.

Orman said nothing as he continued to drink his wine.

"My ambition may be of use to you in the future if you can arrange for me to take my rightful place as clan leader."

"You think that I have the power to do that?" Orman asked.

"I do, my lord," Dunstan said, smiling.

Orman stood at the edge of a tidal marsh as a lantern in the distance signaled that the rowboat was approaching. Dunstan wrapped his cloak more tightly around his shoulders against the damp sea mist.

He turned to Orman. "Why did you ask me to arrange this transport? The displeasure of your king cannot be so great that you must flee his wrath."

Orman replied, "I leave of my own free will. It is time."

"What shall I tell the others?" Dunstan asked.

"Tell them nothing," Orman cautioned. "Swear those men to secrecy on pain of death. Or, better yet, have them killed."

Orman watched Dunstan's eyes dart toward the flickering lantern.

"You are an ambitious man, Dunstan, lurking in the shadow

of your flawed uncle. I predict that in time, your future will have more worth than his."

Dunstan nodded. "Your boat approaches. I will not ask you where it takes you."

"Wise," Orman answered, "for that would make you more complicit. I can tell you only that a time is coming when you or your uncle might be forced to make a choice."

"What kind of choice?"

"A choice of loyalty," Orman answered, and smiled at Dunstan's puzzled expression, noting the boat that had moored on the flat.

Orman added, "And when the time comes, I want you to bring me the Womara woman Seanna."

"I don't understand," Dunstan said.

Orman turned to him. "You do not need to. You need only be prepared. War is coming."

THE STORY CONTINUES...

Coming Soon!

THE BLOOD OF WARRIORS

Stay posted for future updates on book three and sneak peeks.
Visit me at JLNicely.com

ACKNOWLEDGMENTS

My many thanks to:

My brother Douglas, my forever supporter. It is such a joy that we can talk for hours about "the story." I write the words, but your intimate understanding and insights to the characters and scenes bring the tale to life in such an inspiring way.

I am indebted to Lisa Hill, my assistant, and a future book shepherdess in the making. We have learned so much together, but without your steadfast dedication to getting it all on track, I would never have made it through the process.

Katelynn Finnie, who provides invaluable team support, and will take on just about anything we throw at her with enthusiasm and an invaluable youthful perspective.

Special thanks to Annie Tucker, who is my editing guru. Annie knows the right amount of praise for a well-written page to a gentle reminder that I can do better. It has been a great collaboration.

The kudos for handling the logistics of putting the book

together go to Brook Warner, of Warner Coaching Inc., and her team who create the finished product.

Lastly, I am grateful to all my family, friends, and new book readers who have given me such positive feedback on the story and keep asking when the next book is coming. You keep me writing.

THANK YOU FOR READING!

Dear Reader,

I hope that you enjoyed *Warrior Rising*: Book Two of the Womara Series, and the continued adventure of Seanna and James. Many of my readers have expressed how much they wanted to know what happened with my central characters. I was also surprised that many readers were very curious about the fate of the nemesis character Lord Orman, and would he get his just due? The last book in the series, *The Blood of Warriors*, will hopefully answer your questions.

As an author, I love the feedback. Candidly, based on some of the reader input I have received, I wrote a background chapter on some of the reasons Orman became the person that he was. So, tell me what you liked, and even what you disliked. I would love to hear from you. You can write to me at jlnicelyauthor@gmail or visit me on the web at JLNicely.com

Finally, I need to ask a favor. If you are so inclined, I would love a review of *Warrior Rising*. Loved it, hated it—I'd still want your feedback. An author hopes their novel stands on its merit, but reviews still have the power to make or break a book.

If you have the time, here is a link to my author page, along with all my books on Amazon:

https://www.amazon.com/J.L.-Nicely/e/B07FB9RRLH

Thank you for again for reading *Warrior Rising* and spending time with me in the world of the Womara.

In gratitude,

J.L. Nicely

.

Printed in Great Britain
by Amazon